TEARFUL PAGES

BY

AZRA MUFTI

RIGI PUBLICATION

TEARFUL PAGES

BY

AZRA MUFTI

Originally published in India

ISBN: 978-93-84314-78-1
Published by RIGI PUBLICATION

777, Street no.9, Krishna Nagar
Khanna-141401 (Punjab), India
Website: www.rigipublication.com
Email: info@rigipublication.com
Phone: +91-9357710014, +91-9465468291

ACKNOWLEDGEMENTS

Publishing a book is not easy, it a combined effort of few people who help you and encourage you to actualize your dreams into reality. Even though I have been writing for more than a decade now, but writing a book was altogether a challenging and daunting task to do. It required patience, perseverance and passion, thanks to Almighty for showering me these three P's.

 I would like to thank my father who has always been a definition of a perfect person for me. His unrelenting faith, trust and belief in me is what keeps me going. My mother who never wanted me to take a broom in hand, instead a pen! Her silent and inaudible prayers have made my tough journey smooth and I cannot bring any lady to her comparison. I pay my gratitude to my sister, Mrs. Sheema Mufti, sister cum mother, my mentor and guide, who has always motivated and trusted my ambitions. Miss Sabeha Mufti, the star crossed love of my life who pushed me hard to write this book. . It would be unfair not to mention the name of my uncle, Mr. Showkat Ahmad Karimi who has always motivated me to achieve bigger and better. I would thank my cousins, my teachers, my friends and all my relatives who bring out the writer in me and motivate me always.

I pay my heartfelt gratitude to Mr. Junaid Mir (owner of May Nine clothing) for his marketing assistance; his powerful business acumen has helped me throughout the journey. Last but not the least, I thank my followers on Facebook who have always encouraged my writings and placed their trust in me.

ABOUT THE BOOK TEARFUL PAGES

This book is a collection of the haunting and painful stories of gender based issues that have crept into the society and morally corrupt our souls. The book covers a wide range of stories that deal with domestic violence, female feticide, war crimes and cyber bullying in different parts of the world. Although the book deals with the fictitious characters but one can relate the stories with their own lives. The main aim of the book is to create awareness among the people about how women face crime in different forms and at various stages of life. The stories are painful, crude and hurtful. Most of the pages will trigger your brain to think but reading merely does not solve the problems, we need to collectively take some actions against the inhuman practices that are taking place in different parts of the world.

This book does not want to defame and demarginalize any particular sect, religion, country or community but certainly tries to highlight the patriarchy and chauvinism that have set the ugly norms in the society.

The book will certainly create awareness about some basic laws that women need to have knowledge about and benefit from their application. The book also mentions some of the basic rights a woman enjoys in this country.

Have a tough heart and read on!

Index

DEDICATION

Dedicated to my family…and every woman on this planet

x

CHAPTER 1

ARE WE REALLY DEVELOPING?

I did not come this far, to only come this far! As I sit, punching the buttons of my laptop, to carve some magic out of my words, I recollect my journey! A journey of tolerance, courage, pain, happiness, success, guilt, hard work and most importantly patience! When I was in my teens, I never thought this journey would be so exhilarating and daunting! I had my own convictions and belief system that made me believe that this planet is safe, pure, harmless and united. But, sometimes dreams break and so do our convictions! To begin with, it has never been easy to live in this world heavily dominated by men! I do not want to sound pessimistic, but this is what the reality is! Unless you are a woman, you can never feel what it means to be one. Wearing pants and letting your hair down by no means makes you an emancipated and liberating woman, there is much more to this hollow concept of emancipation! But, unfortunately all these slogans go to winds when it is time to practice them!

We claim to be the champion of women rights, but if we go by records, it hangs our heads down in shame. As per a survey according to Wonder list, India is the 8th most unsafe country for women .Don't let India's flashy love stories full of dance and songs fool you. India has been under fire for its inhumane neglect of women's rights. This is the pathetic situation that we have landed in, so how can we boast of living in times where woman is safe and secure. No matter how powerful a girl is, No matter how much successful she is, no matter how many achievements she has in her kitty, she will still be a delicate, fearful and docile lady, who lives in the constant fear of maintaining her chastity and character. It is very unfortunate that we are responsible for this contamination in the society. I purposely used the word "contamination" because I am compelled to say so. Seeing the mushrooming cases of rapes, molestations, domestic violence and eve-teasing in our society! I personally have witnessed umpteen cases where women have been subjected to worst forms of physical and mental torture. I once met a girl in a hospital waiting room, hardly in her twenties, she was crying bitterly, when I asked for the reason, she bursted in tears, narrating her gory story of how she was drugged and impregnated by a rascal who fled away! It is hard for me to trust any man because journalism has introduced me to such stories where I believe there is a small monster in every man! The degree of monstrosity may vary, but the monster is there! Well, I may sound like a hardcore feminist, but this is how circumstances have made me.

Every year, I wish I could write something positive and inspiring on international Woman's day, but when I check my databases, the haunting stories of women surpass the inspiring ones, so I have to write and clear the rust off people's mind who think that emancipation is the new trend that has set in. A woman can claim to be emancipated when she gets due respect from her male counterparts and is not just seen a sex symbol. A woman can claim to be emancipated when she is not seen as an outsider by her in laws, when she does not suffer from physical and mental abuses, when she is safe in any other place expect her mother's womb! Having chosen few women celebrities like Aishwariya Rai and Emma Watson as global ambassadors who walk in obscene clothes and talk about woman emancipation is surely not my definition of women empowerment, instead, when a woman is not banned from observing hijaab, when she is not discriminated against her color, when she is not made a victim of male chauvinism, that is the day when emancipation will set in!

CHAPTER 2

ALCOHOL, DRUGS AND MRS SINGH

Life is very unpredictable, usually it never goes as it is planned, and it lands us in various scary situations and problems that we could ever imagine off. But, I truly believe, whatever happens is for a reason, life throws curve balls at us for a reason, all the trials, tribulations, odds and ordeals are meant to cross our paths for a reason, all we need to have is patience. To have an enduring faith is what takes us to the highest levels of satisfaction and tranquility. I remember spending some of the most beautiful years of life in the beautiful city of Chandigarh. Rich in culture and love, Punjab has its own enigma. You have no option but to fall in love with the people and places. During my sojourn there, I had a chance of spending some quality time with Singh family in Jalandar. Mrs. Singh was one of the jolliest and chirpy ladies I ever encountered with. She had a persona of her own, she made atmosphere lively with her presence. We often used to chat over a cuppa and discuss some realities of life. One day she told me about her story which left me speechless. Her story is torn in fidelity, forgiveness and falsehood!!

Our story begins twenty years before, when parents of girl child used to have only one dream: to get their girls married off to decent boys! It is during those days that Preeti (name changed) was forced to tie a nuptial knot with a man; her parents had chosen for her. She was a petite Punjabi girl and attitude was in her veins. Never in life did she compromise on her principles but now she was given a three day long lecture on" compatibility and adjustment with husband "by her kiths and kins! Preeti was very excited about her new life; she had been harboring this dream for a quite long time. She started hunting the best dresses and jewellery for her; she took care of all the miniscule details somehow related to the marriage. The D Day came and she got married. The inception of marriage was satisfactory and she believed that she got the man of her dreams!! Punjabis are very particular about their looks and Preeti was no exception to it. She turned out to be a beautiful bride and started off her new journey on a very positive note. But, as they say falling in love with a fading shadow is sheer stupidity, same happened to Preeti! Soon the path took a gory turn and started unraveling dark secrets. First few months were quiet smooth, but soon things started to change.

One day she was cleaning the room and she noticed something unusual, bottles of stinky alcohol in the closet! Also, some cheap drugs which she could not figure out. It was a heavy blow to her innocence and faith. Never in her life had she seen such a thing before, she was very sure that her husband was not involved in these things but now truth was bitter and hard to swallow. She chose not to speak about this incident to her husband! She engulfed the bitter taste of this incident and continued to perform her duty of "*aadarsh biwi*"! One day her husband came home, fully drunk, in a state of nonsense and contamination! He started demanding things and shouted nonsensically! Preeti was frightened and immediately followed the commands. Her husband lost it and started beating her without any reason and threw her out of the house. She cried, pleaded but all in vain! She spent the entire night outside home barefooted in biting cold and fell Ill. Next morning, her husband without a speck of remorse in his tone ordered her to prepare breakfast! She wept silent tears and got up!!!

The things started repeating and her husband often came home late drunk and gave her a good beating for no fault of hers. After a couple of years, she became a mother of two kids. Even the tender innocence of these kids could not melt the heart of this drunken monster. As Mrs. Singh finished her story, her eyes were moist and full of pain and unanswered questions. I tried to console her but my words were weak enough to bring that lively Preeti back to life. Life changes, people change, things get better but some scars leave a very huge imprint on our lives and we can never shake those memories away, and the good part is that despite hurdles, you have to move on...

P.S: Mrs. Singh was subjected to worst form of physical and mental torture. There are various cases where wives have been brutally thrashed by their husbands and they succumb to injuries. The main culprit in this menace is drug addiction and alcoholism. Punjab, being a hub of drug addiction is losing its sheen due to such cases. Hundreds of lives are affected daily and it is pathetic to see how family values are being lost to these anti social evils. There are hundreds of Preeti's who share the same story and are subjected to this violence time and again. It is high time that government puts a break on open sale of alcohol and address the issue of drug addiction to put an end to such issues.

CHAPTER 3

THE FACE YOU BURNT IS THE FACE I LOVE

Nausheen, a pretty young girl was a dedicated photographer. Since her childhood it was her one and only passion! She loved to capture moments in her superb clicks! Nausheen started to receive offers from various organizations to work as a photojournalist. After scanning the offers, she finally picked up the carrier of her choice!! She also worked as a freelance photographer and thus doubled her income. She started fulfilling the dreams of her parents and provided them with a lifestyle they dreamt of! Nausheen was very ambitious and loved to add skills to her kitty. She had a fire in herself which never stopped to die down. With each passing day, she wanted to explore new things and capture the lively moments. She had a sparkle which often left a positive impact on others. Being young and talented every rival wanted to have a journo like Nausheen!!

Two years passed and she was flourishing in her career. She had her dream job and loads of other achievements to her credit. So far she had exposed many corrupt people with her apt photographs and unintentionally caught many eyeballs! Her fame was growing far and wide and her swot had doubled! One such scandalous project that she had exposed involved a top notch businessman. He was sentenced to long term imprisonment. He developed bitter cruelty towards this girl and his animosity took an ugly turn. He hired some hooligans and planned to teach her a lesson. On the fateful day, Nausheen left for work and the hired hooligans for lust of money threw acid on her face!! She cried, moaned, wept in pain with no sign of relief! She was rushed to a hospital where she was declared to suffer from 80% damage to her face.

Nausheen, an iron willed girl! This incident did not break and shake her courage. She started to fight. It was no doubt a herculean task to fight the miscreants but she never stopped. She mustered all her courage and started an online and offline campaign against all the acid attack victims! The beginning was slow, many people did not want to hear her story, and others heard her sob story but did not come forward for help. Her faith was shaking but it did not break. She did intensive research and approached all the people she could with her hard earned money. Her campaign gained momentum and invited support from many groups! People started showing interest in her story and wanted to help her somehow. She filed a public litigation and successfully managed to push the miscreants behind bars!! She fought and won!! On being asked if she faces any complex, she replies" The face you burnt is the face I love!

P.S: Acid attack, often known as vitriol attack or vitriolage is one of the most brutal assault in modern times. Bangladesh has been reporting the highest number of acid attacks on women. In India, ASFI (Acid Survivors Foundation India) is a leading NGO which provides support services to these victims. Laxmi Agarwal, an Indian campaigner is doing commendable job in this field. She was attacked at the age of 15. She has also advocated against acid attacks through gathering 27,000 signatures for a petition to curb acid sales, and taking that cause to the Indian Supreme Court. Her petition led the Supreme Court to order the central and state governments to regulate the sale of acid, and the Parliament to make prosecutions of acid attacks easier to pursue. There are thousands of Nausheens and Laxmis in our society, but most of them do not display same courage and patience! We need to support them and love them. Globally, there are as many as 1,500 recorded acid attacks each year with more than 1,000 cases estimated to occur in India alone. However, many attacks go unreported because victims are too afraid of stigma to come forward, most of the girls do not get a suitable match and end up leading miserable lives. A special request to all the guys who have a soft corner for such girls, lend a helping hand to such ladies and marry them, mere slogans won't help! Let us begin a change!! A change of thought and conscience!! Also the government should act strict to the miscreants and punish them. Plus they need to regulate the selling of acid!! Think Different, Act Different!

CHAPTER 4

WHERE IS MY HOME?

I cried in pain, perturbed by noise

Lo! My parents hugged me with care and poise!

The above two lines convey my feelings at the time of my birth. We do not remember the most important time of our life that is the moment we breathed our first. Little do we know of the cascade of events that followed it? Our maiden cry, our maiden laugh and the first time we uttered a meaningful word!! No we do not remember anything, but surely our parents do, and how much it really means to them! The stories of my mother about my mischievous acts set off a cascade of imaginary images in my mind! We all do share one thing in common that is our childhood and the memories of it remain buried in the deepest chambers of our heart! Every parent wants their children to have a princely and royal life and they leave no stone unturned in fulfilling the dreams. For boys, the parents are convinced that they will be the masters, no matter what they become, but the girls are taught right from the birth that they have to leave their homes and go to their "original homes".

Now here begins the confusion, I started my write up mentioning how glorious our childhood is, then where from these baseless and idiotic conclusions follow which discriminates a girl from a boy. Does it mean that the place where I spent two decades of my princely life is not my "original home". When I was a child I had a stern belief that there exists no such thing as "gender divide" and girls can be better than the boys, but as they say "glasshouses are meant to be broken" and so did my illusion! As I grew up the fact was served to me right away at different circumstances and it only led to my broken belief and broken wings (I had a theory that all girls are beautiful princesses and have a pair of invisible wings). Now what led to such a drastic change and complete U-turn of mindset? Here begins the story!!!

I have a distinct relative who lives in a remote part of the valley. As I do not want to reveal the identity, for convenience let us name her Aiza (noble). Aiza was born off poor parents thus not with a silver spoon in her mouth. She was the eldest of four daughters and most sensible of all. She passed her matriculation exam and then had to leave her studies, because neither the monthly income nor her parents supported the decision for further studies. As luck could have it, some months ago her parents got her married off to a peasant who was a distinct relative and 15 years older to Aiza. This was a new challenge for a 16 year old girl who was married to a man almost twice her age. But, Aiza was very mature than her age and accepted the challenge thrown to her by destiny. Aiza like a dutiful wife and a good daughter-in-law shouldered both the responsibilities with poise, patience and grace. She used to wake up early, do all the household chores, serve food to family and then go to fields for her routine work. Year after her nuptial knot, she was blessed with a daughter and she began to dream of a rosier life! But her life was not a different one and as a custom she had to face the taunts of her in laws for giving birth to a daughter. Her husband was not supportive as well and when he used to come in evenings, he threw volley of abuses at her and sometimes would also beat her for not taking care of his family members!! Now here let us give a pause to the story and I request my readers to answer my query. So what is with this marriage stuff? You marry a girl, impregnate her, get the privilege of being a father, and then beat her mercilessly for not taking care of your family members? Ridiculous!

Now, coming back to the story, Aiza braved all the odds and began to swallow the bitter pills of life. One day, her husband came home early and ordered her to make tea. Aiza stood up and fainted, her husband nudged her and commanded her to stand up, she, now fragile and frail in her twenties stood up and served him tea. "Can I take rest for some time", she requested. "Oh! Sure, why not", her husband said with a fictitious smile. She got up and as she stepped forward, he hit her hard from behind and she fell down with her belly touching the floor. Blood began to ooze out and her daughter now 3 years old called a nearby hakim, the doctor checked her and conveyed of her miscarriage. Alas! The husband turned monster had hit her so hard that she lost her baby!

Years passed by and Aiza now became emaciated day by day. One day she decided to put an end to this miserable life and filed for divorce. On hearing this, her husband turned red in face. He feared of humiliation and decided for vendetta. He took out his sickle and chopped her hands!! And then exclaimed," you speck of dust, how dare you go against me, now face the music" and left. Aiza fell there in pool of blood for a long time and then disappeared behind the curtains of time forever!!

This is just one story, but there are hundreds of Aiza's in our society. Who cares for them? Is this the way we are treated in our "original homes"? Who will come to our rescue? How difficult is it to understand that women are:

The crown of society, not the sandals you wear!

She is the respect of family, not the garbage you throw!

She is your honor, not the waste in bin!!

At last she is a human being…so pure, so ethereal!!!

CHAPTER 5

HER SIMPLICITY MADE HER LIFE COMPLEX

Marriage is a very pious institution that completes the belief of a person and helps him to make his life easier and simpler. Every person dreams of a perfect and ideal partner and works hard to find a partner who meets the standards set by him. With difference in convictions and priorities, many people have myriad criterion that they put forward while searching for a partner. For some, beauty is the most important criteria they put forward in their" bride wanted" list. For some, an intellectual connection and compatibility is must. For others a perfect partner consists of a person with good understanding and caring nature. So, different people do have a lot of expectations from their partners and they consider themselves really lucky is they find such a mate! My story is of a girl who had same dreams and expectations as every girl of her age had. Seerat (name changed) lived in the picturesque village of Bandipora district, a teacher by profession; she was a girl of simple living and high thinking. We hardly find such girls in present generation dominated by plastic and artificial beauty. Her simplicity was her biggest asset which saved her from various unnecessary temptations and ostentations.

As luck would have it, she got married to a handsome young man who society thought was good looking than her. She never took these things to heart and started off her journey on a very positive note. She tried to make her journey very smooth by being a perfect wife and daughter-in-law. Her husband seemed to have some issues with this marriage. He usually tried to avoid talking to her and kept himself busy with other things. It pained Seerat to see all these things happening to her which she never imagined off. Still she tried to forget the sourness of her husband's attitude and kept on nourishing this fractured relationship. But, life can be very unfair sometimes, for Seerat, things started to take an ugly turn and conditions worsened. Her husband started rebuking her for her simplicity and he usually passed sarcastic remarks on her looks. He often had the audacity to tell her that he married under compulsion and that his love interest was some other girl. With each passing day, a part of Seerat died and she found it hard to smile at times. To add to the agonies of her life, her In Laws too started to show their true colors. They started creating misunderstandings between the two and poisoned the already sour relation.

After a year of her marriage, the things had taken the ugliest turn, her salary was taken by her husband and the vicious cycle of torture never seemed to stop. They started to treat her like trash and never cared for her necessities. The lust for money had blinded her in laws so much that they wanted to keep her just for the sake of her money. Her husband started making demands of another marriage as he found hard to live with Seerat. After a long pause of tortures and silent screams, Seerat was sent back to her home by her husband. It came as a big blow to her parents who had spent huge chunks of money on her marriage and dowry. Seerat found very hard to live with this reality that she was rejected just because of the way she looked! Her simplicity, her biggest asset once had become a major blockade in her happy marriage. After a couple of months, she got divorce letters from her husband and it shattered all hopes of her happy marriage.

P.S: I truly believe the major culprit in this story is money; the guy married Seerat for the sake of her money, even though he had no liking for Seerat, instead had a liking for some other girl. The love of money blinded the guy so much that he failed to measure the consequences of their marital life. Instead, he should have uprightly rejected the marriage proposal and saved her life. Too often we take hasty decisions and land in the most undesirable and bitter situations. There are many cases like this because greed has taken over humanity in present era. Had the guy taken a stand and convinced his parents not to get him married to Seerat, things would have been different. After marriage, he should have tried to work things out and not tease Seerat for her simplicity and looks. He proved that he lacked integrity and character. It is very important to carefully choose your partner according to your priorities.

CHAPTER 6

CHOICE BETWEEN CAREER AND MARRIAGE

I remember myself wearing a Lab coat in chemistry lab, during my school days and experimenting with Kipp's waste feeling elated, dreaming of becoming a doctor some day, well I lacked ambition those days (sorry, but it is my way of perceiving things), Somehow I landed somewhere else and became a writer both by choice and chance, but this story is not about me and my dreams, it is about a lady doctor, a doctor whose heart wrenching story would leave you drenched in tears by the time you read this whole story! It is a proud moment for all students especially their parents if they turn out to be child prodigy and be a member of this elite cream of the society. Same was in the case of Nusrat (Name changed), she was the only child of her parents and exceptional at studies as well. She, with her swot and sweat made it to the list of successful candidates who qualified MBBS! It was a gala day for her family and they thanked the Almighty for her remarkable success. She also received a gold medal for being a topper throughout the course. She started practicing and opened a clinic of her own. Years passed and many prospective suitors asked for marriage, finally her parents got her hitched to a guy from the same profession, who was an oncologist.

The problem with the guy namely Sabeer was that we was too conservative, money minded, orthodox and regressive at the same time. After their marriage, he put forward a long list of demands to be fulfilled including Nusrat leaving her job. Nusrat could not bring herself to fulfill all the nonchalant demands, but then she was a mature lady and had to surrender to these demands. Sabeer grew irritable day by day and used to take out sheer frustration of his work on Nusrat. Nusrat, once a strong, independent and career oriented woman had to oblige as she was mother of two sons, she did not want that the black shades of their marriage should fall on her sons!

She left her job and used to Baby Sit the kids, in the mean time, her parents started showing resentment towards this decision of Sabeer, but the outcome was even worse, he gagged her phone and strictly forbade her to talk any of her relatives, especially her parents! This was something totally unacceptable! Nusrat now blaming the shady fortune of hers suffers from several disorders and Sabeer is too busy in making a living, that he does not pay any heed to her. Now, after hearing this story, was confidence was in tatters! A girl will always be a girl, an object of tolerance and patience that is it. Now this is a scenario seen mostly in Kashmir these days, Men want to marry highly qualified ladies and then make them sit at homes. What is the point in searching for doctorates and officers when you only want your wives to be your slaves? Stop being so orthodox and callous and give your wives equal rights! And you have no right to shun her freedom of talking to her parents, you are not her owner, just remember that!

CHAPTER 7

FINDING CALM WITHIN CHAOS

"It may have escaped your notice, but life is not fair"-

Dr Seuss If we pay attention, our lives are far from perfect; it is a warehouse of broken dreams, wishes, desires and longings. Some dreams that got shattered with the passage of time, some wishes that remained wishes only, and some desires that inundated with the storms of life. No one seems to be content, there always seems to be a void in our hearts waiting to be filled. But there is a weird sweetness and pleasure in this imperfection. If we try to live with this chaos, fewer conflicts will occur. Our story revolves around this concept, finding the calm within chaos. Saira (name changed) lived in the small hamlet of Kupwara. She was fifteen when she lost her mother to renal failure. Unable to bear the loss of her mother, Saira's life took a U-turn, she completely forgot to live the life she once enjoyed, and she withdrew herself from all social contacts and found solace in solitude. Her father thought of getting Saira married to a guy whom he knew very well. Within few days, Saira was married to Iqbal.

Iqbal, a lawyer by profession, was much older to Saira. He mostly used to visit town for his work and came home on weekends. Saira was very much moved by new changes in her life, she had hardly come out of the trauma of her mother's death, that a new relation started to grow in her garden. Being quiet young, Saira was unable to be a perfect marriage material kind of girl, which heavily troubled Iqbal. Iqbal wanted Saira to leave her life style and live life according to his wishes, he tried to force things on Saira and snatch her independence. Saira was too young to accept these changes, sometimes she even failed to understand, and why she was living with a man she had no compatibility with. There seemed to be a clash of ideas between these two. This often lead to heated arguments and ended up Iqbal cursing Saira and throwing volley of abuses at her.

Many times, Saira tried to talk to her father about this matter, but he seemed to pay no attention towards her agonies. He believed his duty towards Saira was over and feigned fake console towards his daughter. There was no one left in this world to which Saira could spill the beans of her unhappy marriage, she tried to forget the daily abuses and live life without any expectations and hopes. Iqbal, on the other hand had no soft feelings for his wife, he used to come home, take his meals and engage himself in other activities. He never tried to speak to his wife and clear out the bitterness that had crept in their marriage. One day, Saira was doing her chores and Iqbal came. He had brought a lady with him and both of them entered the house ignoring Saira, on being questioned who the lady was; Iqbal in a very loud tone said that," she is my wife and take good care of her". Saira did not know how to react, she wanted to go back to her home, but she knew there was no one to listen her sob story, she wanted to cry, but tears failed to come out of her eyes, all she could do was remember her mother and cry silent tears. She thought Iqbal would now divorce her and send her back to her father's home, but he had sinister designs within. He kept her with him saying that she was a full time maid without even salary so how could he let her go! In Islam it is permissible to marry four women but only if you are sure that you will do justice to all of them, Iqbal did no such thing; he crushed the innocent teen years of Sairas life by making her swallow the bitter pills of life.

Saira, on the other hand found solace in her prayers, she mostly used to sit on a prayer mat and talk to her creator. She also used to give sermons to small kids who lived in the surroundings, in this way Saira found calm in her troubled life. She no longer complains to anyone except her creator and has accepted life as it is without any regrets.

CHAPTER 8

THE UGLY FACE OF SURAT

When I was a little girl, I never thought there is a huge difference between what we see and what actually the scenario is. For me world seemed to be a fine place with simple and serene living. Never did it appear to me that the real world is very hard and difficult to survive with. The people living in it often wear masks and hide their real faces behind these masks. Inside every person we know, there definitely is a person we do not know. I do not want to sound like a pessimist, but the growing crimes, violence, wars, deaths and destruction validate my point. Man's hunger for lust and money has become so insatiable that he can drop down to any limit to meet his evil needs. The worst sufferers of their lust have been the women folk who have seen the darkest phases of life as a result of the violence done on them. At one point of time, it becomes too difficult for a woman to trust her close acquaintances due to reported stories of crime where the criminals turn out to be the closest friends or relatives. Such breach of trust leads to the most deadly mental violence ever inflicted on a woman. Our story revolves around such breach of trust and deception.

Manisha, 24 year old woman lived with her brother in the chaotic town of Surat. Their parents died a long ago when Manisha was hardly seven and her brother Rajesh was ten. Having faced a lot of troubles in their childhood and doing all kinds of menial jobs to support their living, both the siblings had a very troubled childhood. When they were supposed to laugh and play, they used to sell newspapers on roads, this had affected their personality a lot. They believed that the only thing needed for a successful living is money. After Manisha crossed her twenty fifth year, Rajesh got her married to a guy whom he knew quiet for some time. Shekhar, used to work for a very meager amount of money in a sugar industry as a sweeper. He found it very hard to make his both ends meet but after his marriage to Manisha, they managed to earn few thousands more. Manisha was a very skilled woman, she could do all kinds of jobs from cleaning to tailoring thus supplemented her family income.

Due to the growing financial instability in the year 2008, most of the industries went for downsizing, with Shekhar's company being no exception. He was thrown out of the job and here started all the problems. Shekhar moved from pillar to post in search of a job, but no company wanted to go for extra labor due to financial constraints. After a rigorous search for a month or so, he lost his hopes, he used to sit at home and take out his frustration on Manisha. He used to speak a very foul language that could put any vulgarity to shame; Manisha knew his mental condition and chose to ignore his abuses. One afternoon, two of Shekhar's friends came to visit him; they chatted for a quiet long time and took Shekhar along with them. On his return, Shekhar seemed to be calm than he was in the past one month. It soothed Manisha too to see her husband in a good mood. Next day Manisha was busy in kitchen and Shekhar was having his morning tea, in the meantime, his friends who had visited the day before came again, they talked to Shekhar in a very low tone, Shekhar signaled them to go inside the room. Few minutes later Shekhar sent Manisha to that room with tea for his guests. When Manisha entered the room, Shekhar locked it from outside and left the home. What happened to Manisha that day could neither be penned down nor thought off? She was pushed into flesh trade by her own husband for a good amount of money. Manisha talked to Rajesh, a drunkard and drug addict, but he seemed to show no interest, he told Manisha to obey her husband as they were short of money. This incident continued for few weeks and Manisha finally escaped to run from her house one day. She approached some NGO'S who promised to serve her with justice. But, the mental torture she had suffered in all these weeks was insurmountable.

P.S: Human trafficking and sex trade, two aspects not entirely covered in the Justice J.S. Verma panel report, have been linked to crime against women in the cabinet note which suggests "clients" visiting brothels be recognized as offenders who, on first conviction, can face a jail term of anything between three months and one year or a fine in the range of Rs 10,000 to Rs 20,000 or both.

Getting caught the second time would mean a jail term of one to five years and also a fine between Rs 20,000 and Rs 50,000. The ITPA amendments also propose to increase the punishment for maintaining brothels from a jail term of one to three years to three to five years. Although the penalty for first conviction for trafficking remains the same (rigorous imprisonment between three to seven years and a fine of up to `50,000) (Source: Wikipedia).

CHAPTER 9

FRIENDS TURNED FOES

Few months ago boxing legend Muhammad Ali passed, his death was widely condemned throughout the world, his quotes laced with wit and wisdom are such a turn on. They push people to the highest level of motivation. One such quote of Muhammad Ali that has always been a gentle reminder while making social contacts is: I told God to keep me away from my enemies and suddenly I started losing friends. The biggest blessing that a person can ever ask for is having true friends. They are the family that you get to choose in this world. But what if these friends turn out to be your biggest foes? What if they break your trust to extreme and push you to the darkest realities of life. Let us read and find out!

Sahil and Suhana were childhood best friends. They had been together for a pretty long time and they were inseparable. They held mountains of love and care for each other in their hearts. They sat together, studied together, played together and grew together. Their parents were aware of their friendship and they had no qualms about it. They thought both of the kids got along very well and are very compatible with each other. Gradually, they began to grow and their friendship got stronger with time, they used to go to college together and used to study for exams also. Suhana used to prepare notes for Sahil who was not much interested in studies; he had a passion for photography and wanted to make his name big in the photography world. Both of them were passing through a very delicate age: teenage, in your teens, your hormones do all the thinking for you, same was with these two, and they used to have silly tiffs and suffered from usual teenage complexes.

Sahil had a very close friend Amir, who had strong feelings for Suhana, he wanted to vent his emotions but he never found a proper outlet to do so. He usually used to stalk her on various social networking sites and followed her on many sites but Suhana had no clue of his feelings. She never responded to his requests and this hit Amir's ego. Amir knew Sahil and Suhana were very close friends, he now thought of using Sahil as a pawn for getting close to Suhana. Days passed and things were still the same, one day Amir called Sahil and disclosed his feelings for Suhana, Sahil was infuriated on hearing this he told Amir to stay away from her. Amir told Sahil if he helped him he would pay him a handsome amount and also get him DSLR camera which was a dream for Sahil. Sahil did not say a word and left. He did not speak about this incident to Suhana. After few months life started to become very hectic, both of them got very busy with their lives and hardly talked to each other. The bond between them had started to weaken due to no communication. One day, Sahil was travelling from home and he met with an accident, he was riding a very fast bike and it was starting to get dark. He lost grip of his bike and rode fast crushing an old man to death. Having no idea what to do, he left in fear leaving the old man behind. Amir who belonged to an influential family came to know about it. He started blackmailing Sahil for the same; he told him that he would inform the police about this matter if he did not help him getting close to Suhana. Sahil was in dilemma, he did not want to spend the rest of his life in jail nor did he want to do anything that would bring disgrace for Suhana. Amir kept blackmailing him and tired of all his threats, he arranged a meeting of Amir and Suhana at a secluded place giving false information to Suhana that he wanted to meet her. When Suhana went to the given address by Sahil, she was shocked to see Amir instead, she tried to return, but Amir had an ego bigger than mountain itself, he tried to molest her and had hired a guy to shoot it. Suhana was not successful in trying to flee away from the place and started to cry, Amir made her to inhale chloroform which made her unconscious and sexually assaulted her, after some hours, he left her there and left. Suhana gained her consciousness and ran away to her home; she was crying bitterly cursing Sahil and Amir. Next day Amir uploaded this MMS on all social networking sites and tarnished the image of Suhana. On seeing this Sahil was perturbed, he felt sorry for his behavior but he could do nothing about it. Suhana got depressed and was sent to rehabilitation center for some months.

P.S: Under The Information Technology (Amendment) Act, 2008, Cyber-terrorism is punishable with life imprisonment. Cyber offences such as identity theft, cyber-stalking, cyber harassment, spoofing and hacking are the punishable offences under this section. The IT (Amendment) Act, 2008 was passed by both Houses of Parliament on December 23, 2008. Maximum numbers of cyber criminals are arrested from north India. These crimes have increased at a very alarming rate, it is very important to make sure that your accounts are safe and unknown and fishy people do not have access to it.

CHAPTER 10

LOST CHILDHOOD

Summer will end soon, so will childhood~ S. Martin

Childhood undoubtedly is the most beautiful part of our lives. We live every moment in innocence and true spirit without any ostentation. Everything we do speak of real and genuine feelings, far from being unreal. We cry the most honest tears, we smile the most real smiles and we speak the most honest thoughts. To put it in a nutshell, childhood is the most serene part of our lives. But, it is very unfortunate that most of the people do not get this chance to cherish the most loved part of their lives. They are put into such gory situations where they lose their innocence and childhood which dramatically affects their personality. Readers guessed it right I am talking about child marriages, which continues to remain a big blot on Indian society. According to the Indian law, it is a marriage where either the woman is below age 18 or the man is below age 21.These marriages are prevalent in India mostly because people have some socio economic issues. Either they want to get rid of the responsibility or they have some stereotypical misconceptions that prompt them to do so. Naira, a girl aged 12 was a victim of this social evil. She was brought up in the disturbed environs of Patna, Bihar. She wanted to study but her parents wanted her to go to her "home" as it was her final destination.

Naira was too young to understand the concept of marriage, for her it was altogether a new and confusing scenario. When she was dolled up as a bride, she really enjoyed all the attention she got and the way she looked, but deep down in her thoughts she had no idea what was happening around. She landed in her new home hoping to go back to her parents after few days, but this story was new for her. The guy she got married to was thirty five years old. He was given repeated warnings by village heads not to impregnate Naira as she was very young and delicate. Talib was a very rough and crude mannered man. He had little or no regards for village heads; he did not pay any attention to their repeated warnings. Talib's mother was a very wise and generous lady; she had sympathies with Naira and hatred for her parents. She often used to ask Talib why they married her off at such a tender age not knowing that her son had paid them huge amount in return. She used to teach new things to Naira which she learnt very quickly. One day Naira was in kitchen and suddenly puked out. Her mother in law called for a local doctor and examined her, she was pregnant!

Talib was overjoyed to hear this, his mother was very upset with how the things turned out to be, she had a feeling that things are going to worsen in future. Talib used to get lot of fruits and eatables for his 12 year old pregnant wife, he often told her that she has to give birth to a boy else he will not spare her. One day, Naira was climbing stairs, her foot lost hold and feel, and she was immediately rushed to the hospital and suffered a miscarriage. The doctor told them that she should be taken care off well and her body is too frail to bear the weight of a child. Talib was infuriated; he developed a sudden dislike for Naira. He used to come home late and mistreat her. One day he remarried a girl and brought her home, his mother was shocked to see this and told him to leave the house. Talib cursed Naira for casting a spell on his mother. The new couple left the house and went to live in nearby locality. Naira was growing and her mother in law turned mother took very good care of her. She sent her to the nearby school and both of them lived peacefully.

P.S: the Government of India brought the Prohibition of Child Marriage Act (PCMA) in 2006, and it came into effect on 1 November 2007 to address and fix the shortcomings of the Child Marriage Restraint Act. The change in name was meant to reflect the prevention and prohibition of child marriage, rather than restraining it. The previous Act also made it difficult and time consuming to act against child marriages and did not focus on authorities as possible figures for preventing the marriages.[1]This Act kept the ages of adult males and females the same but made some significant changes to further protect the children. Boys and girls forced into child marriages as minors have the option of voiding their marriage up to two years after reaching adulthood, and in certain circumstances, marriages of minors can be null and void before they reach adulthood. All valuables, money, and gifts must be returned if the marriage is nullified, and the girl must be provided with a place of residency until she marries or becomes an adult. Children born from child marriage are considered legitimate, and the courts are expected to give parental custody with the children's best interests in mind. Any male over 18 years of age who enters into a marriage with a minor or anyone who directs or conducts a child marriage ceremony can be punished with up to two years of imprisonment or a fine. (Source: Wikipedia)

CHAPTER 11

THAT UNEXPECTED JOURNEY TO BROTHEL

Destiny is immune to scrutiny, we as humans do not know what is going to be the next phase in our life, there are a lot of twists and turns that occur in our life. Sometimes we plan the things but nothing goes according to that, destiny punches us hard sometimes and it becomes hard to realize whether we are living in a real world or hallucinating. Every next phase of your life demands a better and confident version of you! We make short term plans and long term plans but one incident changes everything and puts a kibosh on our plans, no matter what you have to get up, dress up and face the music and dance to the beats of life. You are not a tree or mountain you have to make moves to be alive. This is the spirit of life, no matter what, you have to move on!

Suhani, a very bright and beautiful girl completed her masters in Business Administration, she passed with a distinction and was very much positive about her future. She had very high goals in life, she wanted to get some experience with a job and then start a business of her own. This was her childhood dream; she always wanted to be an entrepreneur! After she completed her degree, she started hunting for jobs. She got some offers but they did not suit her profile, day by day she was losing her confidence and thought of doing some other online courses. She updated her biodata on all job portals and spent most of her time in mailing CV's to reputed companies. One day she got a call from a consultant for an interview, it came as a breather to her, and she prepared herself well for the said interview. Next day she went to the particular consultant for interview, she put on her best smile and confidence; she entered the office and could see a man in his mid thirties sitting on the other side of the chair. The interview lasted for more than twenty minutes and she was offered a job in Delhi.

She had no fears of doing a job in National Capital as she had been to various cities before and lived on her own. She packed her bags and left. On reaching there, a person was waiting to pick her up from the airport as promised by her consultant. They left the place and headed towards the hotel where she was supposed to stay for a day. On reaching there, she was directed to go to the room specifically booked for her; she went to the room and rested for a while. Few hours later she could hear some noises; she came out of the room and saw a very disturbing scene, this so called hotel was a brothel instead where girls from different regions were tricked into trafficking by giving them fake lucrative job offers. She was made to inhale some strong gas and fainted. When Suhani regained consciousness, she saw herself in a dingy room with a fat, aged man. She cried and pleaded him to spare her; he was indifferent to her screams and gave her a good thrashing. Suhani's parents, clueless of her whereabouts informed the police who took a week to trace her. They arrested the consultant and put a raid on that hotel. All the biggies of this ugly trade got arrested and more than 30 girls were released. They went back to their respective homes, some went to rehab and few others ended up having worst mental disorders.

P.S: Due to growing unemployment in the nation, people are doing very miniscule jobs for money, others like Suhani have to shift to some other cities, it is the responsibility of parents and victims to carefully study the background of people who promise them jobs and inform the police about same. The Government of India penalizes trafficking for commercial sexual exploitation through the Immoral Trafficking Prevention Act (ITPA). Prescribed penalty under the ITPA – ranging from seven years' to life imprisonment – are sufficiently stringent and commensurate with those for other grave crimes. India also prohibits bonded and forced labor through the Bonded Labor Abolition Act, the Child Labor Act, and the Juvenile Justice Act. Indian authorities also use Sections 366(A) and 372 of the Indian Penal Code, prohibiting kidnapping and selling minors into prostitution respectively, to arrest traffickers. Penalties under these provisions are a maximum of ten years' imprisonment and a fine. Bonded labor and the movement of sex trafficking victims, may occasionally be facilitated by corrupt officials. They protect brothels that exploit victims, and protect traffickers and brothel keepers from arrest and other threats of enforcement.

CHAPTER 12

DOWN WITH DRUGS

When life gives you thousand reason to cry, hold on to that one reason that makes you smile. When life throws curve balls at us, it is for a reason. The reason is to make us emotionally strong. Most of us do not know how to handle these tricky situations and lose our battle with life. It is never a smooth sail, everyone has his share of bitter and sour experiences, we have to believe in the fact that no one can claim to have a perfect life. Sometimes the grass seems to be greener on the other side because it is fake, we have to be smart enough to make out what is true and what is not. Sobia was one such person who never lived in a dreamy world; she had always been a tough girl since her father's death and was smart enough to handle tough situations. She was often known as "iron lady" by her peers as her determination and convictions were strong enough.

After completing her senior secondary examinations, Sobia wanted to join an engineering college, she worked very hard to earn a seat in government colleges and thus save her mother from any unwanted expenses. Sobia worked hard enough and was successful to get a seat in one of the colleges she wished off. She left for a sojourn of four years to earn the title of "engineer". Life started to show new pictures to Sobia, She started to pick some fights with people due to her outspoken nature; she was often ridiculed and teased by others for being a poor girl. Taking the advantage of her messy situation, some spoilt students feigning fake friendship started comforting her, they played truancy with her and used to give her drugs, she had no idea why she lost her senses on taking those " calcium rich supplements" that were given to her by these people. Unfortunately she was becoming more addicted towards these with each passing day, she became a drug addict. Due to peer pressure and stress of studies, she found temporary pleasure in drugs, at some times, when she ran out of money, she used to do menial jobs like completing assignment of others and preparing notes in exchange of drugs.

Far from this chaos, her mother had no idea of what her daughter was up to, she was praying and hoping for her better future, after a gap of six months, Sobia returned home, her mother was surprised to see her, she was no longer hale and hearty Sobia, instead she had turned into a zombie, thin and lifeless. Sobia made every effort to be normal but as an addict you cannot act like one. She hunted for ways when she could escape from her mother's vigil and inject herself with drugs. Unfortunately when she was supposed to have broken toys and pens, her closet was full of broken syringes. Pressure and anxiety had made her do so, unable to overcome her addiction, she was trying to do drugs when her mother caught her red handed, it was a piercing situation for her, she did not say anything and just snatched the thing from her. Her mother was a wise lady, she knew reacting or thrashing Sobia would only worsen the situation, instead she took a bold step, she consulted various health consultants and rehab centers, she finally managed to give some support to Sobia, after two months or so, her condition got better, with mother's love and care, she was able to overcome her addiction, now the question was, how to stay safe in future also, she never wanted to leave her home but her mother wanted her to complete her studies. Sobia moved to college for her exams, this time iron willed and strongly determined not to fall to such traps. Fortunately, she used to stay close to her mother and report each situation and thus lived a better life.

For Readers: NDPS (National Drugs and Psychotic Substances Act) views drug offences very seriously and penalties are stiff. The quantum of sentence and fine varies with the offence. For many offences, the penalty depends on the quantity of drug involved - small quantity, more than small but less than commercial quantity or commercial quantity of drugs. Small and Commercial quantities are notified for each drug.

The penalties for various offences under the NDPS Act are as follows:

Offences	Penalty	
Cultivation of opium, cannabis or coca plants without license	Rigorous imprisonment-up to 10 years + fine up to Rs.1 lakh	
Embezzlement of opium by licensed farmer	Rigorous imprisonment -10 to 20 years + fine Rs. 1 to 2 lakhs (regardless of the quantity)	
Production, manufacture, possession, sale, purchase, transport, import inter- state, export inter-state or use of narcotic drugs and psychotropic substances	Small quantity - Rigorous imprisonment up to 6 months or fine up to Rs. 10,000 or both. More than small quantity but less than commercial quantity - Rigorous imprisonment. up to 10 years + fine up to Rs. 1 Lakhs. Commercial quantity - Rigorous imprisonment 10 to 20 years + fine Rs. 1 to 2 Lakhs	
Import, export or transhipment of narcotic drugs and psychotropic substances	Same as above	
External dealings in NDPS-i.e. engaging in or controlling trade whereby drugs are obtained from outside India and supplied to a person outside India	Rigorous imprisonment 10 to 20 years + fine of Rs. 1 to 2 lakhs (Regardless of the quantity)	

Knowingly allowing one's premises to be used for committing an offence	Same as for the offence	
Violations pertaining to controlled substances (precursors)	Rigorous imprisonment up to 10 years + fine Rs. 1 to 2 lakhs	
Financing traffic and harboring offenders	Rigorous imprisonment 10 to 20 years + fine Rs. 1 to 2 lakhs	
Attempts, abetment and criminal conspiracy	Same as for the offence	
Preparation to commit an offence	Half the punishment for the offence	30
Repeat offence	One and half times the punishment for the offence. Death penalty in some cases.	
Consumption of drugs	Cocaine, morphine, heroin - Rigorous imprisonment up to 1 year or fine up to Rs. 20,000 or both. Other drugs- Imprisonment up to 6 months or fine up to Rs. 10,000 or both. Addicts volunteering for treatment enjoy immunity from prosecution	
Punishment for violations not elsewhere specified	Imprisonment up to six months or fine or both	

CHAPTER 13

AN UNQUIET LIFE AND MARRIAGE

We all aim for perfection, we want to be the best version of ourselves, no one can play our role better than us, no two people are same when it comes to their mental set up and thought process, and people differ in their perceptions, values and attitudes. This difference somehow makes the society little bit interesting, imagine a society flooded with only bookworms, or a society full of adventurous lot, there will be nothing special about it, in order to be interesting, things have to be different and each component has its own beauty. Author Veronica Roth writes in her book Divergent," what makes you different makes you dangerous! Our story is about a woman who was totally different from rest of the lot. Zofeen was the only child of her parents, from a very early age, she lived in her own thoughts and dreams, and she had a very different take on life, for her life was a challenge which has to be overcome with sheer hard work.

She had a troubled childhood though; she found it very hard to adjust with people and live up to their standards. She found it extremely hard to strike conversations with people which often made her live a quiet and lonely life, as she grew problems started to bloom further, some days she found it extremely hard to live life normally, other days she was in full blown mania and nothing could stop her from being on top of the world. Her parents had an idea that there was something disturbing about her personality, they tried to consult various doctors but nothing changed, she kept on oscillating between hallucinations and reality. After a rigorous study her father finally decided to consult a neuro-psychiatrist. When she was examined, her parents went in deep shock to learn that she was a patient of Paranoid Schizophrenia.

Her world collapsed, her faith was in shambles, her persona had been given altogether a different name" schizophrenic"! Thoughts of future started troubling her; she could never lead a normal life and could never have a happy marriage or no marriage at all. She finally managed to find a suitable guy who claimed to love her and tied the nuptial knot with him. Both of them knew this was not going to be easy but Zameer assured her he would never leave her. First few months of marriage were quiet normal where the duo smoothly sorted their life problems and tried to overcome the negative impacts. But soon, problems started to erupt, Zameer started to exhaust due to the repeated attacks and weird behavior of Zofeen, she tried her best to be normal, but it was all in the wiring of her brain, she had no control over it. There were times, when she turned violent and hit Zameer but later repented on her actions. Fed up with her routine life Zameer sent her to a mental asylum, she was not insane, just a little bit different from rest. She was completely normal but for her hallucinations, what hurt her most was Zameer giving up on her and sending her to asylum instead of caring and loving her when he had promised to do so. Soon Zameer married one of his colleagues and stopped contacting Zofeen, she came to know about his marriage and this time it appeared someone had plucked her heart and left a cold dark place instead! She tried to make repeated calls to Zameer, not once did he respond. Zofeen had warned her before their marriage that she was not a easy woman to live with, but Zameer was too swayed by her charm that he forgot to take note of the consequences there off. He failed as a husband and worsened the mental condition of Zofeen. Zofeen found herself crying silent tears between the walls of asylum and Zameer lived a normal life. Now a patient of dementia, Zofeen has lost her memory, the only thing she recognizes is the ring given to her by Zameer as a wedding gift!

P.S: Most of the marriages between a mentally ill wife and fit husband end in fiasco. The husband, unable to bear the panic attacks of his wife finally leaves her and looks for some better options. It is important to discuss mental health issues before entering into a marriage contract as it heavily tells upon the lives of people, most of the diseases are even genetic and should be discussed with neuropsychiatrists in anticipation of marriage.

CHAPTER 14

WHERE IS MY DIGNITY?

A couple of years ago, I made a journey from Chandigarh to Kashmir. It was 7 pm and the atmosphere was eerie; I travelled through the busy market of Sector 17 in Chandigarh and compared the night life here and back in Kashmir. Kashmir is dark, quiet and silent place by 6 pmand here the situation is altogether a different one. People take a stroll through the lanes with their family members and enjoy the weekends at different food outlets. Here the situation is quite opposite. Deserted lanes, empty streets and closed shops, this is our Kashmir during night hours.

We kept on walking and as luck would have it, my slippers battered and I had to search for a new one. For a moment, all the weird thoughts of travelling bare foot came to my mind, but luckily a shoe shop lay closeby. I hurried to the place and my hunt for a new pair began. This is one of the difficult tasks for me, as I am not more of a shopaholic. I felt like an Alice in her lost wonderland. I could see many cute and girly slippers neatly stalked. More I explored the store, more difficult it became for me to choose a pair for me. Luckily a friend of mine assisted me and I managed to buy a cute pair of pink comfy slippers. My hunt ended and I made my way to home. I was deeply exhausted and slept peacefully that night. The next day, I was in my study when father directed me to follow him. Clueless about where he was taking me, I followed him blindly. I started to get apprehensions about this stroll. Did he just come to know about the spilled milk? Did he just check my unfinished heap of books in library? Finally my imagination came to a halt.

He headed to the shoe rack and showed me the same slippers. I narrowed my eyes for a pensive pondering and noticed an image of a girl on the slippers. My father and me exchanged looks and thought for a moment, do women deserve such a place? I stood quiet for the moment and my father did most of the talking blaming the oblivious system and people. I kept looking at the face of woman on those slippers. We shout hollow slogans of woman empowerment, but we never take steps to stop the crimes against women, to stop the discrimination against women. Woman who is the mother of humanity has become a salable commodity and they call it emancipation. This is not the way, women should be treated... stand and raise your voices.

CHAPTER 15

WISH DEATH HAD NEVER COME TO ME LIKE THIS

It is mentioned in Holy Quran that every soul should have a taste of death (kullu Nafsun Zayikkun Maut). History bears witness to the fact that whatever has been created has been destroyed. Huge empires, Great rulers, philosophers, religious scholars or ordinary people, no one has escaped from the hands of death. There is no favoritism or gender discrimination in the law of death, but what matters is what our reason of death becomes! Was it natural or planned? Was it an accident or murder? Was it sudden or prolonged? Safoora had never imagined she would become a victim of homicide. Right after her marriage, she had learnt the fact that her marriage was not going to be a smooth affair given the treatment of her husband but she tried to swallow the bitter pills as many times as she could.

She was married in a very conservative and orthodox family where women were still treated to be inferior to men. She was given a step motherly attitude shortly after she was brought as a new bride in the family. She used to get a daily dose of taunt in breakfast and sarcasm for lunch. She figured out in the few months of her marriage that she was brought in this family just to keep the family tree growing. The males of the family treated women just like child producing machines and they have no respect for her individuality. The males used to come home late, eat and sleep. Females were not allowed to share table with them, they were not allowed to talk except for one lined answers. These things suffocated Safoora who was an educated girl and wanted to change this chauvinistic attitude of males in the family.

She tried her hard but all her efforts had gone to winds since there was no change in the attitude of her in laws. After a couple of months, Safoora was expecting a baby, her husband warned her that it has to be a boy (without knowing the fact that it is chromosome Y that is responsible for the gender of baby, and this chromosome is present in males not in females) This chromosome theory was far from their mental comprehension and they lived in fool's paradise to believe that it is woman who is responsible for the gender of baby. The delivery date came and everyone was interested to know whether it was a boy or a girl, the doctor came out of the operation theatre and sighed heavily," we can either save mother or the baby". Her husband got curious to know whether it was a boy or a girl, on shelling out some dollars, the doctor said it was a boy, Safoora's husband got overjoyed and told doctor to save the baby! His family supported his decision. The doctor operated as per the instructions and saved the baby. Safoora died in a pool of blood not knowing that her husband chose the baby over her. There was no remorse in the eyes of her husband. He held the baby in his hands and his chest swelled with pride. Not once did he regret his decision or recalled his wife! How callous a human could be? This reminds me of a line by Khalid Hossaini from his book "A thousand splendid suns" which goes like, *" Man's heart is a wretched wretched thing"*

P.S: In February 2015, a database was launched online entitled" Femicide Census: Profiles of Women Killed by Men". It is a project designed to force recognition of the scale and significance of male violence against women and is the culmination of several years of work by Ingala Smith, who began a grim and time-consuming task of counting Britain's murdered women and putting their names on her own blog back in 2012. There were 126 women killed through male violence that year, 143 in 2013 and 150 in 2014. According to **Indian Penal Code, 1860 Section 304:** Whoever commits culpable homicide not amounting to murder shall be punished with[imprisonment for life], or imprisonment of either description for a term which may extend to ten years, and shall also be liable to fine, if the act by which the death is caused is done with the intention of causing death, or of causing such bodily injury as is likely to cause death, or with imprisonment of either description for a term which may extend to ten years, or with fine, or with both, if the act is done with the knowledge that it is likely to cause death, but without any intention to cause death, or to cause such bodily injury as is likely to cause death.

CHAPTER 16

TAKE MY MONEY AND GIVE ME RESPECT

Marriages are not ugly, people make it so. It is one of the most beautiful and pure form of relation between two people who agree to spend the rest of their life perfecting the imperfections of each other. Imagine how our destiny is written by Almighty and he gives us the right kind of spouse that we deserve at right time, how beautiful is it that the person we spend our life with has been chosen by none other than our own creator! However, keeping the statistics and experience into consideration, it gives me immense displeasure to write that people have totally flawed this beautiful concept. Greed, lust, pride, ego, deception, misunderstanding, trust issues have made marriages complex which otherwise is a very simple phenomenon. We are making this concept uglier day by day, it has been violated so much that most of the people fear at the mere mention of marriage.

Safiya, a very pious and polite girl wanted to have a very simple marriage. She never believed in ostentations and wanted to observe her wedding in a very austere way. She believed that having a beautiful marriage is more important than having a showy wedding. She told her parents to feed poor and give charity instead of making her marriage a huge pomp and show, her parents did as Safiya told them to do, few people were invited to the wedding and *Rukhsati* was carried in a very calm and peaceful manner. No music was played, no photography as allowed and there was no singing and dancing around. She started the new journey of her life peacefully. But, traditions and ostentations have crept into our culture in such a way that it becomes difficult to loosen the grip sometimes. Soon rumor mills started working overtime and set the tongues of people waging, Safiya's simple wedding became talk of the town. Her In Laws too jumped the bandwagon of people who started to raise their eyebrows. They started to taunt her saying that she came" empty handed". Her husband often used to tell her that her parents got rid of her by just shelling out few dollars and handed her over to him.

Safiya was quiet but not blind; deep in the hearts of her hearts she knew that sometimes people do not understand the life we want to live. They want to satisfy their ego by doing illogical and unrealistic things. Problems started to worsen when people started to question about what dowry the new bride had brought with her. Her mother in law used to refer her as "penniless beggar" who had nothing but a ragged existence. Safiya had never imagined in her wildest possible dreams that she would be tortured to this extent just for the sake of materialistic things. She tried to make them understand that she was not in a position to put burden on her parents who had already spent lacks of rupees on her education." We do not want your education, when the only thing you have to do is wash and cook"! They used to tell her. Problems worsened when a nearby neighbor came to their house and offered her daughter's hand in marriage knowing the sourness that had crept into Safiya's marriage. She also offered huge dowry as her own daughter was divorcee. Safiya's husband did not take many days to frame his decision, he divorced Safiya and remarried. Safiya was sent back to her maternal home and she lives with her family.

P.S: According to The Dowry Prohibition Act, 1961: if any person demands directly or indirectly, from the parents or other relatives or guardian of a bride or bridegroom as the case may be, any dowry, he shall be punishable with imprisonment for a term which shall not be less than six months but which may extend to two years and with fine which may extend to ten thousand rupees: Provided that the Court may, for adequate and special reasons to be mentioned in the judgment, impose a sentence of imprisonment for a term of less than six months.

CHAPTER 17

SOME APLOGIES ARE NEVER ACCEPTED

When Amir Khan came up with his jaw dropping movie "Taare Zameen Par" it carried a great message that "every child is special". It raised awareness among common masses that no matter what struggles a child faces in his initial years, he can be a great achiever. Be it a boy or a girl, every child is blessed in his own way and parents should try to harness his talent. There are various difficulties that a child faces during initial years of development and growth but that in no way means that he should be discouraged. However this story is not about any disorder or any movie message, it is about pain and discrimination. It is about tears and fears, loss and regret.

Jasmine was the eldest daughter of her parents, she was a keeper. A very polite and humble girl with a positive attitude towards life. Jasmine always wanted to be a proud daughter of her parents but her love was never reciprocated. Her father always wanted to have a son, he never wanted to father a girl child and since the birth of Jasmine, he always distanced himself from her. There was a void in Jasmine's heart due to the step fatherly attitude her father showed towards her but she was mature enough not to give it the shape of words. She kept her feelings to herself. Due to her equation with her father, her development process was very affected, she never wanted to have a girl child once she got married, she never wanted to get close to anyone knowing that relations are tiring, she always wanted to be the best daughter so that one day her father would pat her back and be proud of her.

Jasmine grew each day with her wounds getting deeper, her father always tried to maintain a distance from her. He never spoke any words of advice to her as fathers are supposed to do. Jasmine tried to make up for the loss in other ways she could, she longed for love, she longed for attention, she longed for care but all she got was ignorance. On her wedding day, when she had to leave her maternal room for ever, she mustered all her courage and went up to her father for a final bachelorette conversation. She entered the room and talked to her father, without raising her eyes she started to begin," dear father, thank you for all the love that you have not given to me for it has only made me strong and powerful, I always wondered why you were so indifferent towards me, is it because I cannot be a support to you in old age, or because I cannot carry the family tree forward or because I was a liability on you, whichever is the reason, I want to tell you that you have given me all the reasons to be angry from God, you have made my days painful and nights lonely, you have given me so many questions which have no answers. Is it the story of every girl? Do their fathers' treat them as a burden? You always blamed mother for giving birth to me but you are equally responsible for the same. As I am leaving today, I feel relived as finally your burden has been released! But, I have only one question to ask, did I really deserve to be treated like this just because I have one extra "S" to the word "He"?

P.S: Jasmine had very painful memories which are never going to leave her. There are still many people around the globe who do not give their daughters the love and care that they deserve. How can one be so ashamed of his own blood? How can man be so selfish? How can he love only those people who serve him purpose and leave the rest? I wonder!

CHAPTER 18

MODERN RELATIONSHIPS AND ROBOTIC APPROACH

It is mentioned in the Holy Quran that Allah created us in pairs. Even before our birth, our destinies are tied to one particular person with whom we would be spending the rest of our lives. Some are very fortunate that they get the person of their dreams in the form of their spouses but in most of the cases our knight in shining armor turns out to be the retard in silver foil! Life is such! No pains no gains. A beautiful life is not easy to build, it exhausts a person, and it is nourished with daily doses of love, care, trust, respect and sacrifice. We cannot envy the happy lives of others without knowing their struggle. We cannot think of living a perfect life without investing in one! Lubna, the protagonist in our story fell in love with a person when she was very young; her hormones were doing all the thinking for her. She found it very hard to vent out her feelings for the person she had genuine feelings for. After a battle of brain and heart, it was the heart that won and Lubna finally disclosed her feelings for Amaar. Both of them entered in the pious bond of marriage after a couple of years of engagement. Lubna was elated as she married the person she loved and for Amaar, he could not have found another girl who loved him in the same way as Lubna did. So it was a win- win situation for both of them.

Amaar had mercurial temper which Lubna was oblivious about but in the few months of their marriage, she had started to get apprehensions about it. Amaar used to get hyper on very petty things and Lubna had no option but to give explanations and teary sobs. But, knowing that Lubna loved him so much, he used to get normal again and apologize for his frequent roars of shouts and anger. Lubna used to sit at home as Amaar did not want her to do job. Lubna never thought Amaar would be so possessive about her but she was so much in love that she was ready to sacrifice her dreams for him. With time, the bond between them got stronger but Amaar failed to reciprocate the same love as Lubna had for him. On few occasions, he used to tell her that he married just because Lubna had feelings for him not because he loved her. These words ripped her heart but she always chose to ignore such stuff and be a responsible wife.

Lubna began to see sudden changes in Ammar's behavior, he used to come home late, often skipped meals, mostly go out for weekend trips and ignore her calls. Lubna complained about these things and Amaar told her she was being a typical nagging housewife. This continued to happen for a good period of three months, not being able to bear it any more, Lubna talked to him patiently. At first, Amaar did not want to confess anything but with repeated requests he put his heart on sleeve. He told Lubna that he never loved her; he found her less attractive and had lost all interest in their marriage. Amaar further told her that he was in love with a girl whom he was dating for a couple of months. Lubna was shattered. Her glasshouse of dreams came crumbling down within seconds. She was lost and numb. Nothing had hurt her as much as Amaar's confession. She went straight into her room and cried. Next day she talked to Amaar and wanted a divorce, she could not spend the rest of her life with a person who was not happy with her anymore! Divorce happened and both parted for good! Lubna is trying hard to forget her ugly yet beautiful past and Amaar has moved on!

P.S: Modern relationships are not build on firm foundation of love and trust, we enter into a relationship just for the sake of changing our relationship status, it is pointless to marry a person for whom you have no feelings, it is equivalent to spoiling two or more lives as such marriages do not work out and end in fiasco. Before committing, one must totally understand the pros and cons of marriage and accept the fact that the other party has to offer. Do not marry when you are lonely but when you are ready! There is a difference!

CHAPTER 19

IT TAKES COURAGE TO BE COURAGEOUS

Small things you say to people makes a lot of difference, little actions you do for others creates wonders, small talks of kindness can weave magic sometimes, it is all in you, all you need to do is just concentrate on that " small change". Sometimes a small change in our mindset, a small idea that pops in our mind and the small revolution it brings can be great. The stereotypes that are prevailing in our society needs to be weeded out at a breakneck pace, the hollow concept of self actualization needs to be lived with full dedication and honesty, all this can happen with a small change! Our story speaks about such change which if adopted can change the lives of many, it can bring back the dead hope of many people, it can enliven the dead souls and spirits and make them live a little better.

Saiqa and suhail was a happily married couple for a good period of two years, theirs was an arranged marriage but the bond between them was so strong that it could withstand any test of time. Their life was running smoothly and with each passing day their concern and care for each other grew more. Suhail was a network engineer and Saiqa after completing her masters chose to be at home and go for various online courses. Both of them had a good understanding, they tried to keep the differences at par and appreciate the similarities between them. It was their birthday anniversary and Saiqa had gone to get some groceries from a nearby store. She wanted to make this day very special for both of them and tried her best to do so. Suhail had taken the car to office and Saiqa had to travel on her own. After getting all the groceries she waited for the cab to drop her home, after a good wait of ten minutes, she finally managed to hire one, as she was travelling she could smell of some obnoxious substance, it was about to make her puke out, she could see the red, drunk eyes of the cab driver, all she wanted was to stop the cab and leave.

She told the driver to stop but he pretended not to pay any attention to her words, he speeded up the vehicle and Saiqa cried for help, she called Suhail but he did not pick, the driver stopped in nearby fields and dragged her out. Saiqa cried for help but no one was there to hear her cries. The driver turned monster was so much drunk that he broke lose all codes of decency and sexually assaulted her. Saiqa was left there to the mercy of God, she cried thousand tears but none could bring back her lost dignity. Suhail called her and all he could hear was teary sobs, he tracked her phone and managed to reach the place where Saiqa was lying, both of them reached home in an eerie silence and terror. They chose not to speak about it for a couple of days, after things started to get better Suhail managed to talk to his wife about it. He made every effort to normalize things for Saiqa but the wounds were too deep to heal so fast, after few days Saiqa got pregnant and the DNA test proved that Suhail was not the father, they could have aborted the child, they could have escaped from the situation but Suhail decided to keep the child! Such a brave and courageous step! Saiqa wanted to abort but Suhail convinced her that it was a gift from God and they have no right to kill any human. Both of them decided to give birth to the baby, such things are rare in our society. Mostly people want to kill such fetus and make life hell for the victim, but if people like Suhail start accepting things, society would altogether change for better. It will save hundreds of lives and victims too will live a respectable life! Think and act!

CHAPTER 20

BLOOD HAS SAME COLOUR HUMANS DON'T

Beautiful meadows, yellow fields, Makki di roti, Sarson ka Saag, pinni and lassi, all these things come rushing to our mind when we hear the word Punjab, one of the richest states of India by economy and culture both. It is a delight to live in Punjab which has a rich cultural background and history. However, what makes you beautiful at times make you dangerous, same is the case with Punjab too, besides having a culture to die for and loving people, and there is a dark side to it! *Haryana* is one of the 29 states in India, situated in North India. It was carved out of the former state of East Punjab. It continues to remain one of the most feared places surrounding Punjab due to some strange customs and traditions followed there. One of the characteristic features of Haryanvis is their Panchayats which are famously known as "KHAPS". Khap is an organization representing a clan or a group of related clans in northern India. Khaps are found mainly among the Jats of Western Uttar Pradesh and Haryana, although historically the term has been used among other communities as well. Sometimes the judgments these Panchayats pass are too tough to handle by local people. Let's read and find out!

Rajan, a young Dalit boy from Sonepat fell in love with a Jat girl Seema. When Seema's family came to know about it, they forcibly married her off to some other guy from Jat community because they never wanted to marry their daughter to a Dalit boy. After her marriage, Seema found it very hard to adjust with her husband because her heart was still in love with Rajan. She made every little effort to talk to him and meet him. Rajan was also very much concerned about Seema and he never wanted her to spend the rest of her life with that man. Both of them met one day and planned to elope from the village to nearby city. This news came as a great shock to both the families and the village as well. They started to hunt them and make them pay for this gruesome act.

After a week or so, they finally hunted them down and were brought to the native village. The Dalit boy was taken in the custody of Jats and was tortured brutally. He was given a third degree treatment for bringing disgrace to the community. Seema on the other hand was grounded and nobody was allowed to talk to her. The case was referred to the Khap Panchayat and they came out with a deadly verdict! They decided that the boy's family should be dishonored to avenge the brother's deed. They decided that Rajan's sisters be raped and paraded naked in the village as a revenge for their brother's action of eloping with a married girl from Jat community! This came as a great shock to both the sisters who were faultless. They never thought they had to pay such a huge price for being Haryanvi girls. They moved the Supreme Court against such Diktat which finally came to their rescue!

P.S: In recent times, the Khap system has attracted criticism from groups, citing the stark prejudice that such groups allegedly hold against others. Women's Organization AIDWA has reported cases where the Khaps are alleged to have initiated threats of murder and violence to couples who marry outside of the circle. The Supreme Court has declared 'Khap Panchayats' illegal, which often decree or encourage honor killings or other institutionalized atrocities against boys and girls of different castes and religions who wish to get married or have married.

This is wholly illegal and has to be ruthlessly stamped out. There is nothing honorable in honor killing or other atrocities and, in fact, it is nothing but barbaric and shameful murder. Other atrocities in respect of the personal lives of people committed by brutal, feudal-minded persons deserve harsh punishment. Only this way can we stamp out such acts of barbarism and feudal mentality. Moreover, these acts take the law into their own hands, and amount to kangaroo courts, which are wholly illegal.

— Bench of Justices Markandey Katju and Gyan Sudha Misra

CHAPTER 21

HUMANS SANS HUMANITY

Some countries in the world are so evil that the only thing one can do is grieve and lament over the pitiable conditions. One such country is Somalia, country located in Africa. It is bordered by Ethiopia to the west, Djibouti to the northwest, the Gulf of Aden to the north, the Indian Ocean to the east, and Kenya to the southwest. Going by the research, Somalia has no capable government that can protect its population from ruthless sexual violence. The security forces, that are supposed to protect the people is often accused for violating human rights. According to the rights body in 2014 report titled *"Here Rape Is Normal": A Five Point Plan to Curtail Sexual Violence in Somalia*, women and girls are target from members of security forces. The conditions are so pathetic that women get raped even while going to market or fields to fetch firewood.

Through some acquaintances and virtual contacts, I came to know about a Somalian woman whose story brought tears to my eyes. It would be unjustified if I do not share it with readers. This victim belonged to the Wajadir district of Mogadishu, capital of Somalia. Maheen lived in a camp for IDP (Internally Displaced Persons), she was a mother of four children, the camp did not have a good reputation but Maheen had no option but to live there with her daughters. The initial days were quite normal but soon Maheen started to know the ugly realities of these refugee camps. One night Maheen was asleep and she heard some noises. The thundering voices outside her tent made her panic. The people outside the camp started shouting loudly, Maheen was terrified, and she got apprehensions that something worst is going to happen. She did not move, after repeated noises, the men entered her tent. They were five in number, heavily drunk with terror in their eyes, they came closer to Maheen.

The four men raped her one by one and one of the guards stood outside. The four men tortured Maheen to extreme and the last one stabbed her with the bayonet of his gun! Next day she approached the police station to report against the accident, but she had to face humiliation there, as she stood there telling about the incident, she started to bleed, the policemen without having a grain of humanity gave her a brush and told her to wash it up, Maheen cleaned the floor and never returned back to the police station after this incident, she thought something worst might happen to her and chose to stay silent. After few months of this accident, she was raped again by a group of assailants in her tent.

For Readers: The United Nations reported nearly 800 cases of sexual and gender-based violence in Mogadishu alone for the first six months of 2013. The actual number is likely much higher. Many victims will not report rape and sexual assault because they lack confidence in the justice system, are unaware of available health and justice services or cannot access them, and fear reprisal and stigma should they report rape. According to the UN Children's Fund (UNICEF), about one-third of victims of sexual violence in Somalia are children. Source (Wikipedia)

CHAPTER 22

GREAT CRIMINALS COMMIT GREAT CRIMES

Great stories travel the world without moving an inch. People form perceptions in the form of pages they read and events they experience. Sometimes we have no option but to cry thousand tears about the pitiable conditions of people across the globe, what makes it more painful is that we can do nothing to help them. All we can do is share their grief by being thousands of miles away from them. The story of Haya, an Afghani girl brought tears to my eyes and by the end you read it, you would be all tears. Read and find out!

When Haya was 14, her parents arranged her marriage with a man twice her age. Haya had four sisters and she was eldest. To ease some of their burden, her parents thought it was better to get her engaged. The man she was engaged to had no plans of marriage yet. He evaded the issue of marriage and did not give them a proper date. Haya was happy in her home oblivious of the destruction that would soon befall her. After three months of her engagement to Saif, one day they heard him shouting outside their home. He had blood all over his clothes, he dragged Haya out of the house to take her with him, no marriage had taken place but he insisted on taking her with him. He kept Haya in a dingy place for two months and mostly tortured and raped her during this period. He was involved in some crimes and hiding from police, and brought Haya with him only to satisfy his lustful desires! Haya was very thin and emaciated and being a minor, her body started to grow weak with each passing day. After two months, a simple wedding took place and Saif took her to his home.

Saif had criminal records and therefore he could not find a job, he mostly stayed indoors and tortured Haya in all unimaginable ways. He hung her up by her hair and stuck hot pokers in her body. He broke her legs and ripped out her finger nails. At the age of 16, she looked like a 60 year old woman. The only happiness she had through these dark times was that of her son, his gurgling laughs soothed all her troubles. Saif did not change his ways, he continued to beat her, one day he was so beastly that Huma got hospitalized. After discharge, she pleaded her mother to take her home; she was taken to her maternal home to get some breather. After three days, her brother in law visited her and requested her to come back, he assured her that things will be normal from now and Saif will mend his ways. Haya believed him and went with him. But this was the biggest mistake of her life. Saif did not mend his ways and turned more beastly than ever. He dug a grave for her in the backyard and planed of murdering her. When Haya came to know about it, she planned for an escape. She wanted to take her son with him because she did not want him to be like his father. She was lucky and managed to escape. She Is now living in Kabul and trying to rebuild her life.

For Readers: **Women for Afghan Women**, also known as **WAW**, is a non-government women's human rights organization, founded in April 2001, which is dedicated to protecting the rights of Afghan women and girls. WAW is based in New York City as well as Kabul, the capital city of Afghanistan. The purpose of the organization is to aid in alleviating the problem of gender-based violence and bring about a change in attitude about the problem. They provide front-line services to women in crisis in eight provinces in Afghanistan. The staff is mostly Afghans and WAW adopts a community-based approach.

CHAPTER 23

CRIMINALS ARE SCARIER THAN CRIMES

Crimes are mostly the same but there are exceptions ofcource, sometimes the criminals are more scary than the crime itself, crime is something that is cosmopolitan in nature, it is not confined to a particular territory or a person, it is pervasive and no matter how hard we try, the growing statistics of crimes show that even the developed countries are a victim of crimes. Let me take you to the place called Cuba, Cuba is located in the northern Caribbean where the Caribbean Sea, the Gulf of Mexico, and the Atlantic Ocean meet. Havana is the capital of Cuba and Spanish is the official language. When I was in high school, I had a fantasy for this place; I loved this name "Cuba", short and sweet and wanted to visit this place one day. Cuba is famous for a number of things like beaches and baseball. But don't make the mistake of jumping on the "Cuba is so safe" bandwagon, sadly due to growing crimes, it is not so safe. Unfortunately several articles of Cuban constitution, the Penal code and other legislation refer to the gender equality, but there are no specific laws aimed at fighting sexist violence, or adequate instruments to protect the victims.

Alshi was accused of being a "jinteran" and was put in a prison specifically meant for them. "Jinterans are young Cuban women who earn a living and support their families by practicing prostitution". Problems did not end for Alshi but started for her. These prisons were the most dreaded places on earth. The accused women were made to work in fields where they were sexually exploited as slaves. In a paper titled, "Situation of Women in Cuba's Prisons" authored by Martiza Lugo Fernandes, the author writes

"Living conditions within Cuba's prisons are inhuman. The punishment cells are just one meter wide by two meters long. Bodily needs must be done in an 8-inch-diameter hole in the floor, located at one end of the cell, through which rats and roaches come in, especially at night. Located over the hole is a 2-inch pipe where water for drinking as well as bathing purposes flows in. Prison authorities turn on the water for just a few minutes and the spray is so strong that it hits the wall and wets everything, including the place where the inmate must lie down. This is nothing more than a concrete slab, very similar to a tomb, with no mattress, sheet or anything else with which to cover oneself during the day.

When the long-awaited family visit day arrives, the inmates are forced to undergo degrading and humiliating strip searches, in which they are stripped naked and searched by several guards. The guards search their hair; the inmates are made to crouch down while nude, to ascertain whether or not they have anything hidden in their private parts; their shoes and other belongings are also searched. Whereas the inmates cannot file any claim denouncing the countless human rights violations committed in the prisons, these measures are implemented even more rigorously in the case of political prisoners, given the fact that these are more aware of what is going on around them

P.S: Be it Cuba or Kokernag, the violence against women in all forms should be condemned. The laws should be made more stringent and the authorities should serve justice to the victims.

CHAPTER 24

I BEND, I DO NOT BREAK

Being a woman is not a thing to be ashamed off but what makes it so is the patriarchal and orthodox mindset of people. There are thousands of victims who have been subjected to the worst forms of violence and crime and what makes it even worse is the justice denied to the victims. In most of the cases, victims do not report such cases to the authorities for fear of stigma, in other cases they have to undergo a long judicial procedure involving huge chunks of money. The result is sometimes victims turn suicidal and commit self harm. One of such stories is that of Ishrat. Ishrat was born and brought up in Muzaffarnagar, Uttar Pradesh. Ishrat was the only daughter of her parents, she was brought up in a cocoon of care and love, her parents loved her very much and she was a shining star of their life.

She was married off to a businessman in a very rich wedding. People were invited on a large scale and both the families exchanged luxurious gifts between them. Ishrat was given a fair treatment in the family; she was shown utmost care and concern by her in laws. Soon Ishrat became very fond of the family and prayed for their happiness. One day she was taking a stroll in the house, she came across a small door which she had never seen before, she moved further and saw it was locked, something within her prompted her to go inside, she tried to get various keys and open the lock but couldn't, finally she got a hammer and broke the lock and went inside. It was complete dark inside; she searched for the lights and bumped into things. She accidently turned on the lights after few attempts. What she saw scared her to the core. She saw a lady in her mid sixties lying on the bed; she was fragile and weak and could barely talk. Ishrat went up to her and talked to her but the old lady kept her eyes glued on Ishrat. Finally she uttered a cry and held Ishrat's hand saying "take me out from here", Ishrat was perplexed, and she did not know what to do. She pacified the lady and told her why was she in such a bad condition. The lady cried and told her she was in beasts who will reveal their true face lately. She told Ishrat not to live in bubble of happiness as the members were beasts in human garb.

As both of them talked, Ishrat's father in law came and shouted in anger, "who brought you here", Ishrat could not speak, he grabbed her hand and took her out of the room, the lady cried, "leave her". She was taken to another room by her father in Law where he in a fit of anger sexually assaulted her. Ishrat was shaken, she was left unconscious. Her beastly father in law directed servants to take her to her room. When she gained consciousness, she was in her room where she saw the same man who had earlier raped her. Ishrat was furious and wanted to shout at him, the monster in front of her silenced her forcibly. He told her not to reveal this incident to anyone otherwise he would put her with the lady in that small room. Ishrat cried and was left alone in the room. Next day, Ishrat crept silently from her room to see that lady again. She went up to her and cried, both of them pacified each other. The lady told her, she was also assaulted by this man and when she tried to raise voice, she was silenced, she further revealed that the men in this family were no less than beasts that exploit their daughters in law and then throw them into rooms to silence them. It had happened earlier with the lady and she had not spoken to anyone in years. Ishrat could not believe the glasshouse of her dreams was broken, she spoke to her husband, but he did not pay any attention to her words and slapped her instead. The reality of this ugly household was revealed to Ishrat and she was left helpless and broken.

P.S: being raped by your own Father-in-law can be a serious blow to one's respect and innocence. Victims of such cases find it hard to live normal lives. The torture and mental pain they suffer is insurmountable. What pains more is that victims find it hard to make others believe what actually happened to them, the accusations are often proved wrong and they are denied of justice!

CHAPTER 25

THE UGLY PENDEMIC

I was fortunate enough to get in touch with a friend who works in a Lab in Haiti that deals with Women's reproductive health issues. She often talked to me about the devasting earthquake of 2010 and how it had affected the lives of people there especially women. She told me how gender based violence has emerged as a grave problem in post earthquake settlement camps. According to Amnesty International 2011, the pathetic conditions have forced many to perform sexual favors in exchange of basic necessities. She narrated to me the heartbreaking story of Sandra, whose family got badly affected in floods and she was made to work as a domestic help in one of the households. In Haiti, the unfortunate children, known as **Restaveks**, are traded into other households by their families, exchanging the children's labor for upbringing. Sandra started to work as a Restavek into a rich family and thus relieves some of her parent's burden. She was just 14 when she started to work in the household; she used to do almost all the chores from cooking, cleaning to dusting. All she wanted in return was education. The kind of favors she got in return was tormenting. Her boss, the head of the family used to rape her quite often. She was not allowed to speak to any of her family members.

Sandra got pregnant within few months of working, the members could feel the change in her physical appearance and was taken to the doctor, the gynecologist told them that she was very weak and giving birth to this child could cost her life. She was brought back to the house and made to work mercilessly. When she was no longer able to do any sort of work she was sent back to her parents. On seeing her condition, they decided to send her to the lab where various health issues were discussed. The doctors in the lab suggested that she should give birth to the child as aborting it could lead to various complicacies. They decided to keep it but it was not easy for them given their crumbling financial position. When time of her delivery came, the doctors declared the baby was born dead and could do nothing to save him. Sandra was taken back to her home and kept there for a good period of two months. After that, her boss came again demanding to take her back as he had paid the money for her, she was taken back by her captor and faced the same trauma that she had suffered before.

She used to face verbal abuse also, her individuality was shattered, her confidence was in tatters, and her life was crumbling. She lost her childhood to the ugly lustrous desires of her captor; she cursed herself for being a girl. She secluded herself from others and often lived in isolation and oblivion. How she wished she had lived a normal life! How she wished she had never been subjected to this form of torture and abuse!

P.S: A UN Security Council study in 2006 reported 35,000 sexual assaults against women and girls between 2004 and 2006. The UN reported in 2006 that half of the women living in the capital city Port au Prince's slums had been raped. United Nations peacekeepers stationed in Haiti since 2004 have drawn widespread resentment after reports emerged of the soldiers raping Haitian civilians. The 2010 Haitian earthquake caused over a million Haitians to move to refugee camps where conditions are dangerous and poor. A study by a human rights group found that 14% of Haitian households reported having at least one member suffered sexual violence between the January 2010 earthquake and January 2012. Sexual assaults in Port au Prince were reported at a rate 20 times higher in the camps than elsewhere in Haiti. (Source Wikipedia)

CHAPTER 26

JUST A LITTLE

When your body is exploited violently, you never remain the same person you had been. Sometimes you feel that you do not belong to the world. These words were narrated to me by a Jamaican Woman who had been the worst sufferer of sexual abuse and violence. Melissa lived in Kingston, the largest city and capital of Jamaica. From a very early age, she had a liking for painting. She used to paint beautiful pictures of meadows and forests and was so much in love with colours. Little did she know that her own life would turn colorless one day. When she was 18, she met a guy online and they developed some serious relationship. Two of them seemed to share a common bent of mind and their discussions usually consisted of Picasso and Leonardo Da Vinci. After chatting online for a couple of weeks, both of them decided to meet and share their paintings.

On the appointed day, both of them showed up at the decided place and time. Melissa met Mandy for the first time and was immediately swayed by his good looks. They discussed about a number of things and left after an hour or so. Melissa started to develop stronger feelings for Mandy who seemed to reciprocate her feelings. They usually met on weekends and used to discuss various issues in their life. One day Melissa got a call from Mandy that he had met an accident and was bleeding profusely. She jotted down the address and left for the place. On reaching there, she could not find any hospital; instead there was a small cottage. She thought it might be a prank call and left, when she turned, she received a heavy blow on her head and was left unconscious. When she gained consciousness, she saw herself tied in chains on a chair in a small wooden room. She could see from her narrowed eyes that Mandy was in front of her. She widened her eyes and shouted. "What the hell is this"? Mandy did not answer any of his questions and slapped her instead. Having no clue of what was going around, Melissa was quiet, after few hours, Mandy came and showed her a video clip. It was Melissa's which was captured by Mandy while she was unconscious. He had brought some goons along and they used Melissa as bait for this clip. Melissa was numb, her clip had gone viral, Mandy had used her for money, and she was still not able to accept the reality.

Melissa was kept there for few days, she was given food which she refused to take, she was made to pee in front of the goons who used to laugh loudly and click pictures." After few days, another girl was brought and same thing was done to her. Both the girls shared their story and came to know that Mandy used social networking sites to fool girls and then make their clips. One day they tried to escape from the place and after many hurdles they were successful. They took the help of the police and got Mandy arrested. All the people involved in this dirty business got arrested and punished.

P.S: According to the article *'Sexual Violence against Women and children: Just a little Sex'* found on the website of Amnesty International Caribbean, "Sexual assault is the second most common cause of injury for women, after fights, and five per cent of all violent injuries seen in hospitals are caused by sexual assaults." Under the heading 'Sexual violence in the home', the article states, "As elsewhere in the world, women in Jamaica are most at risk in their homes - more than half of all violence against women occurs in the home, and just over half of this is perpetrated by intimate partners. Women are nearly 30 times more likely than men to have a sexual-assault-related injury and the perpetrator is usually someone they know."

CHAPTER 27

THE LAST DESIGN

"You did not get mangoes for me this year?" this was my first complaint to Haider who takes care of our garden and happens to be from Bengal. There is one thing I like about these Bengali people; they are very hardworking and determined. Haider has been working with us for the last six years and he is just like a member of the family. When he told me about his educational background, it gave me goose bumps. Haider was a graduate and also worked as a teacher in one of the schools, but due to some debts, he had to leave his further studies and work as a laborer in this disputed part of the country. Knowing that he was very smart in political matters, I often used to talk about the traditions in Bengal and how the judicial system worked there. Knowing that I plan to write a book on gender based issues, he came up with one of the stories he had known about women violence in his state. I immediately showed interest and he narrated the story.

Konkana was born in Murshidabad, a city in Murshidabad district of West Bengal state in India. The city of Murshidabad is located on the eastern bank of the Bhagirathi, a tributary of the Ganges River. Hasina was the eldest daughter of her parents and was a very passionate architect. She completed her degree from one of the reputed colleges in Bengal and thus ended up getting a good job. Her family was very proud of her, besides being a good architect; she was a good sportsperson too. She had won a national level badminton championship and thus was a rising star. She mostly worked on projects that needed her utmost attention and time and thus had to remain outside her home for frequent visits. Her work was famous and all the major construction companies wanted her to be a part of the project. She was selected in one of such projects and was quite happy about it. She used to dedicate most of her time in the project and was very much excited about the results.

One day she received a phone call and she was told to report at one of the construction sites for design improvisations. She left for the place and reached within an hour or so. The place looked very eerie with no one around and cemented buildings all around. She called on the number she had earlier received call from but no one picked up her call. She got inside the building and saw two men standing in front of her. They uttered a cunning laugh and shouted loudly, in no time few men came out of nowhere and now the total number of men enveloping her as nine. She tried to make an exit but they circled around her laughing and making noises. She told them what they wanted but they did not answer her questions. She was blindfolded by one of the men and taken by force. What followed next was totally inhuman and barbaric. One by one, nine of these monsters raped her and shut her eyes and mouth. One of the men received a call and said," *Kaam hogaya sir"*, it made million things cross her mind. "Who could this be? "Was it any of her rivals? Had it anything to do with her rejected proposals? But the pain and shock she was going through could not help her dig answers for her questions. She was taken by one of the men and he left her at a deserted place. She had left her phone somewhere and could not even move her hands. Few hours ago she was seen by some people who helped her gain consciousness and was taken to the hospital. The next day she was taken home and this time her parents were not happy to see her. The shining star of their life had lost all her sheen in a day and their hopes were dashed by the grisly act of monsters that had played truancy with her for few bucks! She left her job and now remains stuck in her room with no interest in the outside world and thus world lost one of its promising architects!

P.S: West Bengal was ranked third in crimes against women, according to the Crimes in India 2013 report released by National

Crime Records Bureau (NCRB). According to the 2012 NCRB report, 30,942 crimes were committed against women. However, the figure has fallen marginally to 29,836 crimes in the 2013 report. According to the report, undivided Andhra Pradesh and Uttar Pradesh ranked first and second, respectively.

CHAPTER 28

THE VENDETTA

Lenisha was always a chirpy young girl who lived in her small happy world. When she was fifteen, she was sent to a boarding school in the picturesque state of Dehradun, she was of Nepali origin, but she was very much excited about her new life in Dehradun. On her first day in school she made friends with a girl namely Mannat. Mannat was a serious looking studious nerdy girl totally antagonistic to free spirited Lenisha. As they say, opposites attract, so did both of them. They started to eat study and live together and became very much fond of each other. One day both of them were studying in a classroom when a group of stout, rowdy boys came to the class and started harassing the juniors. They even tried to make fun of Mannat's gigantic glasses; Lenisha could not take this and shouted at them. All the students started cheering her for her brave step. One of the guys among the group came forward and warned Lenisha that he will make her life hell from now. Lenisha pushed him and threw him out of the class.

Mohit started to harbor hatred for Lenisha, the way he was treated by Lenisha in the canteen always reminded him of his lost "stud image" among the fresher's. He somehow wanted to take revenge from Lenisha. He started to harbor various plans to get his vendetta. Lenisha, on the other hand had no such thoughts, she had even stopped thinking about the incident. One day Lenisha and her friends were eating lunch in canteen when Mohit approached to them, he told them he was sorry for his past behavior and wanted to make peace with them. Lenisha told him that he should be very careful in future and she has no interest in developing friendship with him. But Mohit did not give up, he used to follow Lenisha and Mannat every day, they tried to talk to the school authorities but could not muster the courage to do so. As the school annual day approached, all the students got busy with the practice,

Lenisha participated in the oratory competition, one day she was rehearsing in the class room and Mohit came along with his friends. They shut the door and started harassing Lenisha, he came closer to Lenisha and forcibly kissed her, his friends filmed a video of his act. Lenisha was petrified, she slapped him and pushed him away, soon after this incident Mohit started to blackmail her.

Leisha went to the concerned class teacher and told her that Mohit was harassing her, the teacher on the other hand showed her the video that his friends had grabbed and she snubbed Lenisha for this shameful act. Everybody started to talk about these two, Mohit was enjoying the attention he got but it broke Lenisha, everybody started to talk about her and looked down on her, she cried enough but could not get back her lost respect. She planned to go back to Nepal and leave everything behind. She called her parents and told them to take her along. On reaching back to Nepal, Lenisha was a changed girl, she was not fearless anymore, and she used to get scared on very petty issues and lost all her confidence. This is how a small act of childish behavior completely changed her perception about life and people.

CHAPTER 29

MIRACLES DO HAPPEN

Jannat and Owais were happily married for a period of two years; they were very much in love with each other and valued their relation a lot. Jannat was a very decent girl and even though Owais could not give her the happiness of being a father, she still loved him with all her heart. Her relation was so strong it could withstand all the hard trials of life, most of their close friends suggested to have a surrogate child or an adopted one but Jannat did not want to hurt the feelings of Owais in anyway. She used to tell him to believe in God's plan and wait for the miracles. Both of them used to go for regular check-up's and take all the medicines on time. One day a reputed expert in the related field visited the town and both of them visited him for an appointment.

The doctor seemed to be a very nice person and told them not to worry. He checked both of them for a pretty long time and gave them some hope. He further told them that they can have a baby if they take all the precautions suggested by him, having new hopes in their mind both of them went home happy than ever. Jannat was very tired due to the routine checkup and slept off. After a week or so she started to have a puckish feeling, she ate less and slept less, Owais could not figure out the problem, he felt it was the side effects of medicines she was taking. One day Jannat was doing some chores in kitchen and she fainted, Owais got nervous and immediately called the doctor, the doctor checked her and told them that Jannat was pregnant. Their joy knew no bounds; they could not believe their luck and called all their relatives and friends. Both of them had a very happy time together. But, Jannat's joy was short lived; she was not able to figure out how was it possible just after one visit to the expert. She thought hard. When Owais came home, Jannat talked to him about the matter, she told him when the doctor checked her she was unconscious for an hour and after she got up she had a very aching and different feeling. Owais was terrified on hearing this shocking revelation. Was it that doctor had tried to commit some crime? Was he responsible for the news they had received? Was it not Owais's baby? These questions caused tsunami in their minds. However, they took an intelligent step; they did not go straight to the doctor and instead called up the police.

The police investigated both of them and went up to the doctor. On seeing the police and both of them he was petrified, the fear in his eyes cleared all doubts, it was he who had made both of them unconscious and sexually assaulted Jannat on the pretext of check up. The police arrested him and grabbed the CCTV footage that he had forgotten to remove. He was sentenced to Jail and penalized heavily. Jannat and Owais reached home heartbroken, their happiness was lost in the bubble of the moment. However, they decided to keep the baby and considered it as a part of God's plan. Both of them started a happy life.

CHAPTER 30

THE HIDDEN HURT

Some of the most gruesome crimes that the history has ever witnessed have unfortunately been a part of some hideous tradition. The problem with a typical and orthodox society is sometimes they fail to use logic and believe what their forefathers make them to. One of such crimes that are still practiced in some parts of the world is FGM (Female Genital Mutilation). The World Health Organization defines FGM as "the partial or total removal of external female genitalia, or other injury to the female genital organs for nonmedical reasons." The procedure is usually performed on girls before puberty, between the ages of nine and

13, and has no health benefits. Most of the people still believe that for a girl or woman to be 'clean,' 'pure' and 'feminine,' she must have her genitals cut at a young age," it states. " Many parents will have their daughters cut as a proactive measure so that they will be 'marriageable' In some communities, men refuse to marry any woman who has not been cut. So strong is the belief that even some girls and young women buy into the validity of the practice."

Gift was born in Ugep, a Nigerian village to poor parents. She was a bubbly young girl with dark black eyes and beautiful hair, one could make out from her talks that she was a gifted child, a rare combination of beauty and intelligence. When she was eleven, she was taken by her mother to an old woman who lived nearby. When gift reached there, she could see a number of women assembled in a room waiting for her arrival, she could not figure out what was going to happen, all she could see was her mother talking to the old woman who was center of attraction. The old woman called Gift and made her lie on the bed, she was confused, she did as she was told, all other woman were signaled to go out of the room and only candles were lit. Gift could feel her genitals were touched by that old woman and she was holding something like scalpel in her hand. Without any anesthesia, the parts of the poor girl were cut and she cried in pain. She was making loudest cries possible but the people in the room were blinded by pseudo faith and ignored her cries.

After few days gift could feel some pain in her private parts and was taken to the doctor, she suffered from a serious infection as the blades that were used for her operation was not clean and hygienic, the poor girl suffered from immense pain but had no option to stay quiet as it was her mother who was responsible for her condition.

P.S: A 2013 UNICEF report found that 27.2 million people had undergone FMG procedures in Egypt – more than any other country in the world. The procedure can cause problems ranging from pain during urination and discomfort during sexual intercourse, to potentially fatal complications during childbirth and psychological trauma. Female genital mutilation is commonly referred to as "female circumcision," but a more accurate term is "female castration" because victims typically lose the ability to become sexually aroused. As a result, they're not tempted to engage in premarital or extramarital intercourse.

CHAPTER 31

HER MARITAL RAPE

When something is packaged in social norms and misunderstood religious ethics, one is conditioned into staying silent even in the face of pain and suffering. It is not necessary that we are in love with the same person we are married to, love and marriage are two different things, sometimes we have to move with the pace of life irrespective of our wishes and dreams, and this is what happened to Raima. Raima was a fiercely independent, outgoing and extrovert girl. She believed in making things happen, she had an aura of liveliness and confidence which reflected in her style. After completing her studies, her parents pushed her into getting married, she wanted to live life according to her own convictions but being born in a highly conservative family, she had to surrender her dreams and wishes. One fine day, she got married to a family friend and started off her new journey.

Raima found it very hard to reciprocate the love and feelings for her husband; she was not compatible with him at all. She found a sea of difference between the two mindsets and this gap was telling upon their marriage. Sumit could make out that Raima was forcibly dispensing off her duties as a wife that further infuriated him, it was a heavy blow to his male ego and as a result he forced things on Raima. There was no such thing as understanding in their marriage and Raima often resisted his desires. Things started to take an ugly turn when Sumit used to beat her for not being physical with him, Raima tried hard to make him understand that she was not happy with him and making love to him was a torture to her peace but he continued making out with her despite her non consent. He used to tie Raima with chains and force himself on her, this is what we call marital rape, and soon she turned into a zombie with no wishes of her own. When you are married to a person, he has very right on your body, but what if you are not at all comfortable sharing yourself with him? Does it mean your spouse will continue seeking pleasure without your consent?

Marriage is for women the commonest mode of livelihood, and unfortunately the total amount of undesired sex endured by women is probably greater in marriage than in prostitution. Use of force and violence for having sex with you partner is something that is unacceptable both emotionally and ethically. If such situation arises in any marriage, both the partners need to talk about this issue and clear it out. It should not hit their ego as it spoils the basic fundamentals of marriage. Unfortunately, most of the women cannot speak about this matter because they are taught from a very early age that husbands are their protectors and owners and they can do whatever they want, but does it mean that a woman has no right over her body? If she has no physical compatibility with a person, how can you force things on her? Time to introspect!

CHAPTER 32

THE MISSING LINK

Not everyone is lucky enough to turn their dreams into reality; some bury their desires deep down into their hearts because they do not find a proper outlet for expression of their wishes and ambitions. Saira always wanted to be an engineer, she had been harboring this dream right from her childhood, she used to build building out of mud and stones and found immense happiness with her creations. After her senior secondary examinations, she expressed her wish of joining an engineering college, the finances of her house did not support her decision, somehow she wanted to motivate her parents and pursue her dream, the only thing her parents told her that is girls do not need to spend so much on their education when the only thing they have to do is get married. Saira pleaded her parents to spend the amount on her education instead of her marriage, but when you live in patriarchy, you cannot expect wonders to happen.

She left her studies after twelfth standard and waited for some unknown prince charming to take her to his own castle. She was married off with the same money that she wanted to spend on her education. She wanted to forget the ugly memories of her unfinished career and focus on her marital life, she used to stay at home for the whole day and waited for her husband to turn up after the late hours, she grew irritated day by day, she wanted to work but she had no such qualifications, she wanted to study further but with a partner like Suhail, it was a tough thing. Slowly she started to realize that Suhail wanted her only to take care of the home without getting paid for it. Her job was no less than a maid in the house who has no powers in the decision making. She started to develop hatred towards life; she started to feel the indifferent treatment that women are being subjected towards in the society.

Her husband started to get fed up with her, he could not support her free ideas, her soul was so wild to be tamed by such fake marriage, both of them parted for good, within few weeks Suhail remarried and Saira started to take classes and pursue her higher education. She dedicated most of her time into studies and also managed to get a part time job also, she engrossed herself so much into work that she forgot all her past worries, in few years, she completed her education and managed to get a respectable job. Her parents who once refused to educate her were now proud of her. They supported all her decisions and Saira proved that it is more important to spend on girl's education than her marriage.

P.S: Most of us still have a patriarchal mindset, we still believe that it is more important to spend on girls marriage than on her education, girls like Saira should come forward and break the barrier of traditional thinking, they should stand up for themselves and carve a niche for themselves in the society.

CHAPTER 33

WELCOME TO GARSTIN BASTION ROAD

A stroll through the lanes of Garstin Bastion road of Delhi popularly known as GB Road serves as a treasure of thoughts for any writer. Also known as the "land of pink nipples", G.B. Road is the Asia's largest and World's second largest red-light district in Delhi, India. It is an area with several hundred multi-story brothels and estimated over 12,000 sex workers, this place is surrounded by stench, exhausted rickshaw pullers and bizarre voices. Being infamously known for prostitution and paid sex, government has failed to give justice to the victims brought their and forcibly made to indulge in immoral activities. Having known one of the stories of victims of such place, I got altogether a new outlook about forced prostitution in India. Sundari was brought to this place at the age of nineteen, she was a college going student and one day she was kidnapped by some goons and left into this hell for never to return.

She failed to make any contact with her parents and they couldn't also trace her out due to the strong network and political support of this area. A field of lust, cruelty and abandoned ladies, Sundari was forced to work in GB Road and serve the lustful desires of the moneyed people who visit this place. The rooms in this place are very small and dingy; the conditions are so unhygienic that most of the girls die in the initial phase of their journey. Sundari survived all the pain, crime, injustice, and suffering and mostly cries silent tears. Every woman deserves to live a very respectable and serene life, but the people like Sundari often fall prey to the vicious cycle of crimes prevailing in the society. Talking at length about the problems she faced at brothels, Sundari had a list of things she wanted to vent out her anger at/ The Dalaals who bring them there are paid in return of their service and are paid " free sex" in return.

The rooms where girls are made to work are full of stench and claustrophobic.

The fat bellied women are the caretakers of the brothel and they make it a point that no one is allowed to escape or refrain from the duties they have been assigned, sometimes the girls are made to work without getting any payment in return. The food they are given to eat is very cheap and mostly girls have to eat very less in order to maintain their figure. The government has badly failed to take any preventive measures to stop the unethical activities that are being carried out at GB Road.

CHAPTER 34

WOMEN, WAR AND PEACE

If you destroy a woman, you destroy an average of six other people with her because she is no longer in a position to take care of others, so in a way you are destroying a huge chunk of population. Women is responsible for keeping the flow of humanity going, but history stands witness to the fact that she is the one who suffers immense inhumanity at the hands of society. Stereotypes, patriarchal mindset still rule our lives and the brunt is suffered by a woman alone. One of the most famous wars to have ever taken place on this planet is Vietnam War of year 2002. Vietnamese civilians were butchered, women and girls raped, and homes burnt, this brings us to narrate the story of Seiri, she was one of the victims of the Vietnamese war who lived in Binh Dinh province of central Vietnam. Her story gives us an insight of what it means to be born into a trouble torn land.

Seiri was held captive by the forces for a pretty long time and during this struggle she faced various kinds of mental and physical abuse. She was made to entertain many men at a time and all of whom were no less than beasts. The grisly attitude of forces towards the victims of the war shook their faith in humanity, there was no one who could hear them, all they could do was to utter silent cries and live dark lives. Seiri was mostly kept in a trench and many people would visit her and raped her again and again. Wars are obscene; one can very well imagine the brutalities that take place without actually being a member of it. Things started to take ugly turn for Seiri and each day she was subjected to a new tragedy, her condition became pathetic day by day and later she was diagnosed with AIDS. She got a life threatening sickness without any fault of hers. Every day became a new tragedy for her; she lost control over her own body.

The children who were born out of such torture and unrest were referred as *lai Daihan*. The term is specific to children born of a South Korean father and a Vietnamese mother. It is unclear how many of these children were born, but estimates range in the tens of thousands. Unfortunately these children were ostracized by the Vietnamese and stigmatized because they were a product of rape and forced sexual encounters. These children were often looked down upon by society and even they had to bear the brunt of war for no fault of theirs.

P.S: From 1964 to 1975, an estimated 1,500 people died during the forced relocations of 1,200,000 civilians, another 5,000 prisoners died from ill-treatment and about 30,000 suspected communists and fighters were executed. 6,000 civilians died in the more extensive shellings. In Quảng Nam province 4,700 civilians were killed in 1969. This totals, from a range of between 16,000 and 167,000 deaths caused by South Vietnam (Diệm-era), and 42,000 and 118,000 deaths caused by South Vietnam (post Diệm-era), excluding North Vietnamese forces killed by the ARVN in combat.(WIKIPEDIA).

CHAPTER 35

WOMEN UNDER SIEGE

A woman with an education may be able to spend more time sitting in a chair instead of lying on her back. A sound advantage, I should think."
— **Anne Bishop**, **Daughter of the Blood**

From times immemorial, women have been facing a lot of discrimination in various forms, the crimes have grown to such monumental proportions that sometimes we forget to state that they are crimes; we have got so much accustomed to the world of terror and violence that our headlines are incomplete without the stories of reign of terror and violence. Violence undoubtedly has taken various insidious paths that any brain can imagine. The sad part is that mostly the victims have to tone down their experiences because of the shame and humiliation that follows after the expression of the assault on them. Our story revolves around the violence that is carried out in brothels on prostitutes. It may cause some people to do the double take but certainly these places are not even safe for the women who work at such places. Julie was brought to a street brothel by some pimp who falsely took advantage of her gullibility. May be the man who brought her there was very much aware of the fact that how much monetary gains she was about to bring.

The first beating Julie got was from an older woman, solid and squat in built, for not being able to work properly, it scared her, she felt a feeling of claustrophobia being treated wildly in that brothel. The second shock came to her when she was told to attend multiple customers in a day as she was much in demand in her initial years. It made a robot out of her; she was turned into a stooge who forgot to laugh at all. Julie tried to escape from this wild place but she was caught by some ladies and forcibly thrown on the floor which broke her front teeth, as a result of this, she was not given any work to do for a week nor any compensation, she was made to do every chore of the brothel to earn two square meals a day.

After a week, she was brought back into the business; she was made to work for hours satisfying the lust of beasts in human garb who have no respect for any women in their life. Life was getting very hard for Julie, she started to suffer from internal weakness and excessive bleeding, she was not offered any consultation till matters got worse and finally was given some respite in form of injections.

P.S: The moot point is that violence in prostitution does not come from one direction, it comes from a variety of directions, and it can come at any time in any form. One needs to take extra care about the pimps who are chiefly responsible for the execution of this business. The government should play its part and completely ban prostitution in whatever form it may be.

CHAPTER 36

VIOLENCE WITH WORDS

Violence against women can be in many forms, it can be physical, emotional, verbal, sexual, economical and social. There can be a blend of different types of violence's too. What needs to be done is to study the pattern of violence's that are taking place and then taking the timely action. Most of the women are denied the right of personal dignity; they have to suffer harassment and exploitation at various situations irrespective of age and status… A number of sociological studies show that young Indian females now prize financial independence, freedom to decide when to marry and have children, and have glamorous careers. The boom in software industry especially BPO's has given employment for not so qualified girls also. Dalit /Scheduled caste (SC) women, in India's highly patriarchal and caste-based society, bear the triple burden of caste, class, and gender. Being positioned at the lowest social order of Indian society, Scheduled caste women suffer from many forms of discrimination, including lack of education, economic disadvantages, social disempowerment, domestic violence, political invisibility, and sexual oppression. In contravention of both national laws and international human rights standards that prohibit any physical, sexual or psychological violence against women, varying forms of violent acts specifically targeting SC women are occurring on a large scale across India today.

Suman was born in Dalit family in Karnal, Haryana. She never knew that she would be entangled into web of caste superiority and orthodox mindset just because she was considered to be of low caste. Her problems started to erupt when her classmates started to treat her inferior and passed unhealthy comments on her. She was treated like an untouchable and was often made a subject of fun to be laughed at. Things became worse when two boys oh her college who were heavily drunk tried to rape her just because she was not deserving to live an honorable life. The physical torture was for few days but the words that were used by the boys for her community went deep into her heart and pained her. The words reverberated in her ears time and again and she had no option but to utter a silent cry every time she recalled those words.

CHAPTER 37

SOME RIGHTS WOMEN NEED TO KNOW

After reading all the stories, the thing that readers need to know is how to fight such crimes and violence. It is a very serious issue and needs to be solved collectively. Every person has to contribute somehow in order to mitigate the losses. The most important of all is to create awareness among the people about such gory crimes and that is the main motto behind writing this book. Women, all around the globe need to stand up for their rights but that is only possible hen they have an appropriate knowledge of their rights. Keeping this concern in mind I have stated some laws and rights forth that every women in India needs to know.

1. Free legal aid: Under the Legal Services Authorities Act 1987, all female rape victims have the right to free legal aid. "Whenever a rape victim is unable to hire a lawyer, it's mandatory for the station house officer to inform the city's legal services authority to arrange a lawyer for her,"

2. Right to protect one's identity: According to Section 228A IPC, all victims of sexual assault have the right to anonymity. Neither the media nor the police can force them to reveal their identity in public. Unpermitted publication of the identity can even lead to imprisonment for the publisher. Moreover, the victim can record her statement with a magistrate either alone or in presence of a lady police officer.

3. Women witnesses can't be called to police stations
Indian women witnesses have the right to record a statement at home. Section 160 CrPC states that women cannot be called over to police stations for interrogation. "If a woman is a witness, she can choose to record her statement at her own residence in presence of a lady police officer,"

4. No arrests at night: According to Supreme Court ruling, a woman cannot be arrested between sunset and sunrise. This was the result of a rising number of police harassment complaints by women.However, if the woman in question is wanted for a serious crime, police can make an arrest with a special permission from a magistrate.

5. Right to maternity leave: The Maternity Benefit Act 1961 ensures 12 weeks of paid leave for a mother, taken before or after the delivery. However, it allows a maximum six weeks of leave before delivery.

6. Right to equal wage: The principle, equal pay for equal work, holds good for any working women. According to the Equal Remuneration Act 1976, no organization can discriminate between men and women doing similar work or having same designation vis-a-vis recruitment or pay.

7. Safety at the workplace: Any workplace with more than 10 employees is duty-bound to create a Sexual Harassment Complaints Committee. According to Supreme Court's Vishakha Guidelines, the presence of such committee is mandatory and it must be headed by a woman.

8. TIME NO BAR: During an incident of sexual abuse, a survivor goes through many levels of emotional and physical stress. There are times when it takes the survivor months before they can finally come to terms with the incident and register a complaint and, thankfully, our legal system understands that. The Supreme Court has ruled that even if there has been a gap between the report and the occurrence of the incident, the police must register an FIR.

9. COMPLAINT VIA EMAIL: If, for some reason, a woman can't go to the police station, she can send a written complaint through an email or registered post addressed to a senior police officer of the level of Deputy Commissioner or Commissioner of

Police. The officer then directs the SHO of the police station, of the area where the incident occurred, to conduct proper verification of the complainant and lodge an FIR. The police can then come over to the residence of the victim to take her statement.

10. ZERO FIR: The concept of a 'Zero FIR' means that an FIR can be filed at any police station irrespective of its jurisdiction to receive complaint. Even if you are far off from the place of incident and may not be sure of the correct jurisdiction, the Station House Officer of a police station is under legal obligation to lodge your FIR. A Zero FIR can be filed at any police station, irrespective of place of incident or jurisdiction, and it can be later transferred to the right police station.

11. RIGTH TO PRIVACY: When reporting an incident of rape or sexual assault, it is of utmost importance that the victim feels comfortable and is not under any sort of mental duress or stress while narrating the incident. The law lays down that it is the duty of the police to upkeep the woman's right to privacy. Under section 164 of the Criminal Procedure Code, a woman can record the statement with only one police officer and woman constable in a convenient place that is not crowded and does not provide any possibility of the statement being overheard by a fourth person, at a location of her choice.

12. DOCTOR'S VERDICT NOT FINAL: A woman has the right to have a copy of the medical report from the doctor. Rape is a crime and *not* a medical condition. It is a legal term and not a diagnosis to be made by the medical officer treating the victim. The only statement that can be made by the medical officer is that there is evidence of recent sexual activity. Whether the rape has occurred, or not, is a legal conclusion and not one that the doctor can decide.

13. RIGHT TO STAY AT NATAL HOME: "Every woman should know the Protection of Women from Domestic Violence

Act, 2005, a civil law that provides protection against all forms of violence and abuse; be it physical, sexual, verbal, emotional and/or economic. One of the reasons many women are unable to escape abusive or violent relationships is that they have no safe space to turn to—the matrimonial home is not theirs and they're no longer welcome in their natal home. Under DV law, not only can you seek an injunction against the violence, but it also recognises the woman's right to reside in the matrimonial or shared household, whether or not you have any rights to the concerned property. Also, marital rape is not codified as a crime in India; however, under DV law, a wife can secure an order prohibiting sexual abuse by a husband.

14. NO CHARGES: In 2011, the Supreme Court ruled that according to Section 497 of the IPC, a woman cannot be preceded for her involvement in an adulterous relationship. In fact, the section says that she can't even be charged for being an instigator of the adultery.

15. DIVORCE: Under Section 14 of the Hindu Marriage Act 1955, a couple cannot register a petition for divorce within a year of marriage. However, if the High Court feels that the petitioner is experiencing immense problems then the former can permit the latter to file for divorce.

16. NO SACKING: Maternity Benefit Act 1961 states that no woman can be sacked from her employment regardless of any reason while she is pregnant.

LAWS THAT ARE MADE FOR WOMEN AND CHILD PROTECTION IN INDIA

1.   Laws relating to women

- Commission of Sati (Prevention) Act, 1987

- Criminal Law (Amendment) Act, 1983

- Dowry Prohibition Act, 1961

- Immoral Traffic (Prevention) Act, 1956

- Indecent Representation of Women (Prohibition) Act, 1986

- National Commission for Women Act, 1990

- Prohibition of Sexual Harassment of Women at the Workplace Bill, 2010

- Protection of Women from Domestic Violence Act, 2005

2.   Laws relating to working women

- Contract Labour (Regulation and Abolition) Act, 1976

- Employees State Insurance Act, 1948

- Equal Remuneration Act, 1976

- Factories (Amendment) Act, 1948

- Maternity Benefit Act, 1961 (Amended in 1995)

- Plantation Labour Act, 1951

3.   Laws relating to marriage & divorce

- Anand Marriage Act, 1909

- Arya Marriage Validation Act, 1937

- Births, Deaths & Marriages Registration Act, 1886

- Bangalore Marriages Validating Act, 1936

- Converts' Marriage Dissolution Act, 1866

- Dissolution of Muslim Marriages Act, 1939

- Family Courts Act, 1984

- Foreign Marriage Act, 1969

- Hindu Marriage Act, 1955

- Hindu Marriages (Validation of Proceedings) Act, 1960

- Indian Christian Marriage Act, 1872

- Indian Divorce Act, 1869

- Indian Divorce Amendment Bill, 2001

- Indian Matrimonial Causes (War Marriages) Act, 1948

- Marriage Laws (Amendment) Act, 2001

- Marriages Validation Act, 1892

- Muslim Women (Protection of Rights on Divorce) Act, 1986

- Parsi Marriage & Divorce Act, 1936

- Prohibition of Child Marriage Act, 2006

4. Laws relating to maintenance

- Order for maintenance of wives, children and parents under section 125

- Procedure to be followed under section 125

- Alteration in allowance under section 125

- Enforcement of the order of maintenance

5.   **Laws relating to abortion**

- Medical Termination of Pregnancy Act, 1971

- Pre-Natal Diagnostic Techniques (Regulation & Prevention of Misuse) Act, 1994

- Pre-Natal Diagnostic Techniques (Regulation & Prevention of Misuse) Amendment Act, 2001

- Pre-Natal Diagnostic Techniques (Regulation & Prevention of Misuse) Amendment Act, 2002

6.   **Laws relating to property, succession, inheritance, guardianship & adoption**

- Guardians & Wards Act, 1890

- Hindu Adoptions & Maintenance Act, 1956

- Hindu Inheritance (Removal of Disabilities) Act, 1928

- Hindu Minority & Guardianship Act, 1956

- Hindu Succession Act, 1956

- Hindu Succession (Amendment) Act, 2005

- Indian Succession Act, 1925

- Indian Succession (Amendment) Act, 2002

- Married Women's Property Act, 1874

- Married Women's Property (Extension) Act, 1959

7. **Laws relating to children**

- Child Labour (Prohibition & Regulation) Act, 1986

- Child Marriage Restraint Act, 1929

- Children Act, 1960

- Children (Pledging of Labour) Act, 1933

- Commissions for the Protection of Child Rights Act, 2005

- Infant Milk Substitutes Act, 1992

- Infant Milk Substitutes Act, 2003

- Infant Milk Substitutes, Feeding Bottles & Infant Foods (Regulation of Production, Supply & Distribution) Act, 1992

- Infant Milk Substitutes, Feeding Bottles & Infant Foods (Regulation of Production, Supply & Distribution) Amendment Act, 2003

- Juvenile Justice (Care & Protection of Children) Act, 2000

- Juvenile Justice (Care & Protection of Children) Amendment Act, 2006

- Prohibition of Child Marriage Act, 2006

- Reformatory Schools Act, 1897

- Young Persons (Harmful Publications) Act, 1956

8. Offences against women and children in the Indian Penal Code

- Abandoning of child under 12 years of age

- Adultery

- Assault or criminal force to a woman with intent to outrage her modesty

- Buying minor for purpose of prostitution

- Causing death of quick unborn child by act amounting to culpable homicide

- Causing miscarriage or miscarriage without the woman's consent

- Cohabitation caused by a man deceitfully inducing a belief of lawful marriage

- Concealment of birth by secret disposal of dead body

- Concealment of former marriage

- Death caused by act done with intent to cause miscarriage

- Dowry death

- Enticing, detaining or taking away with criminal intent a married woman

- Fraudulent marriage ceremony without lawful marriage

- Husband or relative of a husband of a woman subjecting her to cruelty

- Importation of girl from foreign country

- Intercourse by man with his wife during separation

- Intercourse by a member of management or staff of a hospital with any woman in that hospital

- Intercourse by public servant with a woman in his custody

- Intercourse by superintendent of jail, remand home, etc

- Kidnapping, abducting or inducing woman to compel her marriage

- Marriage ceremony fraudulently gone through without lawful marriage

- Marrying again during lifetime of spouse (Also see here)

- Preventing a child from being born alive or causing its death after birth

- Procreation of minor girl

- Selling minor for purpose of prostitution

- Word, gesture or act intended to insult the modesty of a woman

CONSTITUTIONAL RIGHTS OF WOMEN

The rights and safeguards enshrined in the constitution for women in India are:

The rights and safeguards enshrined in the constitution for women in India are listed below:

1. The state shall not discriminate against any citizen of India on the ground of sex [**Article 15(1)**].

2. The state is empowered to make any special provision for women. In other words, this provision enables the state to make affirmative discrimination in favour of women [**Article 15(3)**].

3. No citizen shall be discriminated against or be ineligible for any employment or office under the state on the ground of sex [**Article 16(2)**].

4. Traffic in human beings and forced labour are prohibited [**Article 23(1)**].

5. The state to secure for men and women equally the right to an adequate means of livelihood [**Article 39(a)**].

6. The state to secure equal pay for equal work for both Indian men and women [**Article 39(d)**].

7. The state is required to ensure that the health and strength of women workers are not abused and that they are not forced by economic necessity to enter avocations unsuited to their strength [**Article 39(e)**].

8. The state shall make provision for securing just and humane conditions of work and maternity relief [**Article 42**].

9.   It shall be the duty of every citizen of India to renounce practices derogatory to the dignity of women [**Article 51-A(e)**].

10. One-third of the total number of seats to be filled by direct election in every Panchayat shall be reserved for women [**Article 243-D(3)**].

11. One-third of the total number of offices of chairpersons in the Panchayats at each level shall be reserved for women [**Article 243-D(4)**].

12. One-third of the total number of seats to be filled by direct election in every Municipality shall be reserved for women [**Article 243-T(3)**].

13. The offices of chairpersons in the Municipalities shall be reserved for women in such manner as the State Legislature may provide [**Article 243-T (4)**].

REFERENCES

www.wikipedia,com

https://en.wikipedia.org/wiki/Protection_of_Women_from_Domestic_Violence_Act,_2005

http://edugeneral.org/blog/polity/women-rights-in-india/

http://ncw.nic.in/frmllawsrelatedtowomen.aspx

http://timesofindia.indiatimes.com/life-style/relationships/love-sex/10-Rights-every-Indian-woman-should-know/articleshow/51303660.cms